Vintage Sterling

Vintage Sterling

Mary Beth Walsh
and
Charles A. Witschorik

RESOURCE *Publications* · Eugene, Oregon

VINTAGE STERLING

Resource Publications
An Imprint of Wipf and Stock Publishers
199 W. 8th Ave., Suite 3
Eugene, OR 97401

www.wipfandstock.com

PAPERBACK ISBN: 978-1-5326-4781-9
HARDCOVER ISBN: 978-1-5326-4782-6
EBOOK ISBN: 978-1-5326-4783-3

Manufactured in the U.S.A.

This book is lovingly dedicated to our family and friends, who have inspired us, supported us, and walked alongside us on the journey.

Chapter 1

STERLING SÁNCHEZ KNEW HE had this one in the bag. The night was cool and misty, and he'd had his usual round of drinks downtown. It was late and the alcohol was starting to work its magic. In others, it might have induced drowsiness or stupor, but not so for Sterling. He was a happy drunk, even a courageous one. Nothing like a couple drinks to take away the few inhibitions he had and send him headlong, laughing, into danger.

Tonight was no exception. Feeling no pain while barreling down the deserted, slippery road that lead from L.A. to his secluded rural estate, Sterling was in a mood to kick some ass! His wine-exporting business had never had such a year. A recession may have been gripping most of the country, but people still needed something to console them—a sentiment Sterling himself had affirmed that very day with the new luxury car he'd just bought with cash. Speeding him along the highway at ever greater speeds, it was a new acquisition—a proud addition to his collection of rare, classic BMWs. And now here he was tooling along in his new black beauty, without a care in the world. It seemed like everything he touched these days turned to gold. And he just couldn't allow himself to even think about the bottom dropping out, even though his sixth sense was telling him something was off and doom was just around the corner. *Ha, who gives a damn*, he thought. *I'm on top of the world. Really, who could possibly stop me?*

Best of all, Sterling had all the women—and the woman—that he wanted. He was considered hot, he thought, by everyone he met. Standing just over six feet tall, with a trim, athletic build from years as an award-winning competitive swimmer, he was more than willing and able to hold his own in all areas of romantic warfare. His girlfriend, Tess, was a perfect physical match for him, with her raven hair and sleek, slender body. She was a safe bet, and he didn't mind the security that their relationship brought. He could play around plenty and yet still head home to the safe haven of Tess's arms. She'd been with him since they met in college and had continued with her career in physical therapy even after he'd made his first million. In many ways, Sterling didn't understand why she stayed with him. His trips home were increasingly brief and he knew he wasn't giving her the attention she longed for, and probably deserved. She said she loved him and would never leave him, but really he wasn't too concerned even after what had transpired at tonight's meeting. If she felt like staying, it was fine, but there certainly were others to turn to. Though he occasionally felt an ever-so-slight pang of remorse over Tess, Sterling enjoyed the thrill of the conquest. At work. On the road. And especially when it came to the ladies. There were many occasions and ample opportunities for adventure in the life of an unstoppable young impresario.

That night, in fact, Sterling had just come from a meeting with Tess and other important members of the board of his company, the eponymously named Sterling Enterprises, Inc. Having built the company from the ground up, Sterling was very proud of his achievement and of all the successes he had accumulated as CEO. The meeting that night had been typical of Sterling's free-wheeling-yet-focused approach. Gathering together a group of several dozen important stockholders, donors, and their entourages, Sterling had called the meeting to celebrate the company's latest acquisition. Sterling, Inc. was by now a globally recognized brand, and as its chief executive, Sterling had important clout in the world of the most important vintners, restaurant entrepreneurs, and beverage companies. And yet for the longest time there had been one business he had set his sights on which had not been so easy to win over.

CHAPTER 1

Belonging to his parents, the small-scale, local vineyard called Sánchez Vintage, located in northern California in the fertile, secluded hills of the Santa Cruz Mountains, just south of San Francisco, was a plum target. Sitting in a remote mountain valley, where he'd grown up, and enjoying some of the most favorable wine-making land and climate conditions, the Sánchez business had so much potential in Sterling's mind. His parents, who had inherited the land from his father's family, going back many generations in his Mexican-California family roots, had always seen their business on a local scale—more as a part of the community than as an enterprise with national or international ambitions. Sterling, at least at this new point in his career, saw things very differently. Here was a chance, he thought, to seize an amazing opportunity and incorporate the family business into a company he had already grown at a phenomenal pace. His parents had been against the idea from the beginning, not objecting to the choices he made with his own company, but wanting to stay true to their own approach to the life they'd always known. The "big bucks" and all that goes with that lifestyle was not something they ever wanted. They were simple folks with simple needs. Family and friends were more important to them than the things that money can buy. Certainly they appreciated making a good income that afforded them a comfortable way of life, but beyond that they didn't want the hassle of what comes along with too much fortune.

Still, Sterling wasn't one to take no for an answer. He'd begged and pleaded with them for long enough, and had finally decided to move things along in a way that would secure his objective. Maybe he would have preferred a different method, but he had to do what he had to do. At least that's what had passed through Sterling's mind once again earlier that evening as he surveyed the room back at work, taking in the sight of the guests at the party he had decided to throw, mingling, toasting, and congratulating him and the other board members at their newest acquisition. Cracking a smile with a clever smugness Sterling felt sure he'd earned, he was astonished as he looked out the window at the night sky and the parade of city lights below to see reflected in the glass panes the sight of the elevator door at the rear of the room open, and Tess walk out, staring him down with an expression he could detect, even through the dark reflection of the glass, was anything but happy or approving.

Turning around, Sterling barely had time to start uttering Tess' name before she had made her way toward him, barely containing her unmistakable rage.

"What the *hell* do you think you're doing, you selfish, self-centered jackass?" Tess managed to get out with an intensity that, though not yelling, telegraphed to all present that something was terribly wrong.

"I don't know . . ." Sterling tried to get out a few words, but Tess was having none of it.

"Oh don't even go there. Don't even think about denying what's going on. I mean, how *could* you take such advantage of them and of their trust in you? You know what that land, that place, and that business, mean to them. You know it's all they have. You know it's your *family* that's at stake here. And we both certainly know that going global was *never* anything they wanted for the family business!" Tess did her best to hold in both her rage and the tears she could also feel welling up inside.

"Oh come on, Tess. Let's talk about this some other time, I've got . . ."

"Yeah, I know, Sterling. You've got all the V.I.P.s here. All of your pawns assembled! Ever ready to dutifully present themselves to bow down and worship at the feet of your massive ego. You self-absorbed asshole!"

"Tess, please . . ."

"No, I really don't care anymore, Sterling. I helped you start this business, I've been your advisor, working remotely while I try to build my physical therapy career back home. I've been your friend, your girlfriend, your lover, and your long-waiting fiancée, and I've put up with a lot for the sake of supporting you and our so-called relationship. But no more! This is the last straw. You sell out your family. You threaten them with eviction and legal action as the majority stakeholder in their business if they don't sell out completely to you. Well, good for you. Congratulations on getting all you ever wanted. I hope you enjoy it. You can keep the cash, the fame, the fortune, the connections, the society friends. But in exchange for all of that, you have lost me. I'm out of here and I'm not coming back. Goodbye, Sterling, and good luck keeping the wolves at bay, because you're gonna need all the luck that you can get. Perhaps, someday, you might just realize that you're going to need more than your success and your status and your oversized ego to keep you going!"

With that, and with the party stopped cold in its tracks and everyone around listening with both shock and fascination, Tess bore into Sterling's eyes with a look that could have both killed and broken hearts, slid the engagement ring she'd worn for years off her finger, and grasped it in her hand. Visibly shaking with emotion, she seemed ready to throw it across the room, but closing her eyes she slowly raised the ring, placed it over the glass of high-end champagne Sterling held in his hand, and let it drop, fizzing and clinking, into the glass. Turning around she walked with her head help high to the elevator, stepped inside, and disappeared behind the closing door.

The room remained eerily quiet for what seemed an eternity, all eyes fixated on Sterling and his reaction. Slowly bringing his mouth closed again after staring in shock in the direction of where Tess had walked, Sterling surveyed the room, drew in a deep breath, and cracking a sly grin, exclaimed, "Well, ladies, guess this means I'm a free agent, again!"

With a wave of nervous yet audibly relieved laughter, the room went back to normal, conversations continuing, deals developing, and the future of Sterling Enterprises, Inc. appearing more secure than ever. As Sterling wrapped up conversations that night and sealed more connections, he tried to look on the bright side of things while he fingered the engagement ring he had transferred to the bottom of his suit jacket pocket. Sure, it was embarrassing losing Tess in that way, and no doubt he would miss her on occasion. And yet, to think of all the opportunities that awaited in the future with his company. Other people's moral scruples were not going to stop him, and nor, back in his car, was the speeding night train Sterling viewed on the horizon as he sped on, careening along the highway, high on life and the thrill of an acquisition signed and sealed. Bearing down on the train crossing the landscape in the distance, now outside the city limits, traveling at what seemed to be exactly the same speed as his new ride, Sterling was not about to let this mega steel monster get in his way! Slamming his foot on the accelerator, he raced toward the now-closing gates, ever so slightly gaining on the intrusive locomotive. This was going to be a close one, but Sterling wasn't worried. It was do or die and he wasn't about to give in, not with the roll he'd been on.

And so the gates were closing. Just a few feet away now, Sterling realized he wasn't going to make it under them in time. But he had made the call. He was going to beat this massive thing and, sure enough, he did. Whizzing around the closing gates in a tight zig-zag, Sterling actually felt the blast of speeding air from the train push against the back of his car, as it cleared the far side of the tracks. This had been a close one. Perhaps closer than any before, judging by the sweat-drenched clothes now clinging to his shaking frame. But he'd done it. There was an air of triumph in what he'd accomplished, and he knew he was even more of a badass than he'd thought, even as he felt the sweat drench down his temple. Rocketing through the night air, he was on top of the world, and he couldn't help but look down to see how fast his muscle car was rocketing him forward. 107 mph. Bad! Ass!

And then it happened. His eyes had only glanced down for a brief second to check his cell for a possible text from Tess, yet when he looked up again something was very different. Where just a moment before there had been black pavement and white lines illuminated by his headlights, now there was only brown. It took just a split second for Sterling to realize that the road had not changed color. Before his brain could even process it, he knew that a pack of large coyotes lay directly in his path and that any impact at this speed would kill him and them both. Instinctively, his hands took hold of the wheel and spun it furiously right, narrowly missing the animals but jetting the car instantaneously into a series of rolls too numerous to count. After a mere handful of seconds, the damage was done. Sterling's new speed machine lay upside down on the desert floor, its windows blown out, its wheels still spinning in the night breeze. Sterling dangled inside, his body suspended from a seatbelt and his life hanging precipitously in the balance.

Chapter 2

IT WAS RED. THAT was all he could make out, at first. As Sterling's eyes slowly opened, his head throbbed with shattering pain and he felt the fierce tug of the seat belt stabbing against his abdomen as it held him suspended in midair. Blood from the wounds covering his body dripped haphazardly down his chest and head, forming pools and streams on the now-inverted roof of his car, sparsely illuminated in the reflected glow of shining headlights and framed by the hum of still-spinning tires. But through the fog of his bewilderment and discomfort there was something taking form in Sterling's line of sight. Shapeless and shifting at first view, gradually, as his eyes focused, the image came into clearer perspective.

A face. That much was clear by now. Sterling was staring into what resembled a pair of smiling, kind eyes. The drops of his own blood brought the image into sharper relief as they fell, but to Sterling the face was startlingly real. As he looked into the mysterious, beckoning eyes, suddenly he could feel the scene changing around him. From the inverted position of his body inside the overturned car, his consciousness now transitioned as if to an alternate plane.

Keeping his gaze fixed on the kindly eyes, the surrounding scenery finally came into view. He was in his old room, and it felt like home. Standing in the middle of the bedroom in which he'd slept throughout his childhood, Sterling took in the familiar scene before him. A bed, a desk stacked with the storybooks and adventure tales he liked to read as a boy, a shelf filled with memorabilia from childhood sports teams—including several ribbons and trophies from the school swim meets in which he often competed—all of it framed by a panel of windows overlooking a vast expanse of countryside and sky. It was the vineyard in a remote valley just south of San Jose, California that his parents had inherited from his father's own parents and theirs before, dating back many generations. Long rows of vines stretched out into the distance, ripe for the harvest time he could tell instantly from their size and shape was just a few weeks away. The sun was gently setting over the foothills in the distance, streaming through his window and warming his forehead and arms.

Sterling was just about to turn toward the door of his room, instinctively to head downstairs toward the kitchen and living room, and where he imagined his parents and sister would be, when his eyes met the gaze of the face he had first encountered in the car. Compassionate and wise, he now looked into the eyes and realized they were connected to a body. It was a middle-aged, Hispanic gentleman of medium height and build standing there before him, and Sterling swore he knew him. He couldn't quite put his finger on where he'd seen the man before, but there was an air of familiarity and friendliness about him. He felt as though the piercing stare from the man's striking green eyes would bore a hole through the back of his head. It was almost impossible for Sterling to look away from the hypnotic gaze of this seemingly friendly stranger.

And then the man spoke. "Sterling," he said. "Welcome home." Startled, Sterling felt a jolt of recognition that he was in fact in a place that was comforting and peaceful. And yet, he was not at all sure what it meant or if he could even believe it. He felt as though he couldn't trust his senses any longer and would have to rely instead on instinct to guide him through this confusion.

Incredulous and hopeful at the same time, Sterling asked the man, "Who are you, a ghost?" Smiling, the man responded, "No, Sterling. I'm not a ghost, I'm a friend. I'm here to help you come back."

"Come back?" Sterling replied. "What do you mean? I didn't know I'd gone anywhere."

"You've gone a lot of places, Sterling," replied the man. "But how many of them have you really *been* to? How often were you really there? How much did you actually realize and take in all that was going on around you?"

Sterling wasn't at all sure how to respond, or even what exactly it was that the man meant. But clearly this was a unique opportunity, and he was never one to turn down an adventure.

"I don't know," Sterling finally offered. "But I bet you're going to show me," he quipped with the smug playfulness he had perfected as a business owner and passionate aficionado of the good life. He always thought of himself as the world's best salesman and sometime con artist, with the ability to sell pearls to any oyster in the sea.

The man laughed and said, "You catch on quickly, don't you?"

"Never miss a beat," Sterling replied, relishing his ability to charm. "By the way," Sterling added, "I didn't catch your name."

The man smiled and replied. "Well, I thought you'd never ask. My name is Chris."

"Nice to meet you, Chris," Sterling answered.

"And to see you again, Sterling. You probably don't remember, but we've met before," Chris added.

"Interesting. I don't remember," Sterling interjected.

"Exactly," added Chris. "That's what we're here to do. To help you put it all together again."

Sterling smiled. He had no idea who Chris was or where all of it was going, but he knew somehow it would all turn out alright. And he was going to enjoy the ride.

Before he realized what was happening, the scene suddenly began to change around him. As he tried to discern the emerging sights, Sterling instantly recognized another sensation. Like a window opening into a world both familiar and distant, Sterling felt immediately transported to childhood as he discerned the sounds of his grandfather's strumming guitar and booming baritone voice. Now fully immersed in the moment, Sterling recognized the scene around him. He was outside at evening in the back of his family's farmhouse, the moon beaming gently down on the spreading rows of vines and a small fire burning in the outdoor hearth. Sterling remembered viscerally where he was as he took everything in. Though it was clear that he couldn't be seen by anyone, he found himself in a familiar place—in fact, one so familiar that he was startled to recognize none other than himself at what must have been age seven or eight. There he was, surrounded by his family, sitting enthralled as his grandfather, *abuelo* Alfonso, shared the songs he had grown up singing.

His grandfather was the family's connection to a legacy that went back many generations, all the way to the time when the land stretching out before them had belonged to Spain, and later Mexico. Since at least the early 1800s, Sterling's family, through his paternal grandfather's ancestors, had lived on, worked, and eventually owned the land they now called their own. Though his grandfather was a quiet person, he never hesitated to express to Sterling and his other grandchildren the pride he took in their heritage—in the legacy they had received from those who came before. For *abuelo* Alfonso, there could be no better way to express that pride than through song, especially the traditional folk songs of Mexico that he had learned as a boy and shared with his wife, and Sterling's grandmother, Lupe. Originally from Jalisco, Mexico, Lupe had made her way north with her own family as a girl to work in the California farm fields that relied on the hard work of so many migrant laborers, and still do. By coincidence, at one point many years before, her family had happened to be working in the area of Alfonso's farm, and as destiny would have it, the two met and struck up a romance that would soon lead to marriage and a family. Lupe too had grown up singing the songs of rural Mexico, the melodies of love, loss, hope, and humor.

The older Sterling smiled as he observed his younger self swaying and humming along with the music. It would only be a few years later that his *abuelo* would pass away, and it touched a place deep inside him to be in Alfonso's presence once again. Often since his passing Sterling had wished he could go back and see his grandfather again. He knew Alfonso had told him stories about his own youth and about their shared ancestors. He knew there had been so many things both of his *abuelos* had passed on to their grandchildren, and yet it was all too easy to lose track of the contours of those memories as time went by.

What Sterling did know was that Alfonso and Lupe were the last link the family had to the old traditions. In fact, Sterling recalled that he owed not just his life and culture to his grandparents, but his very name. As he observed the scene before him, he smiled to watch his grandfather strum as the nostalgic tunes poured forth, it seemed effortlessly, from somewhere deep within both himself and the guitar. Focusing in more closely on his grandfather's strong, seasoned hands, he could easily make out the telltale sign of Alfonso's playing—a small silver coin he used instead of a pick as he strummed the chords of each song. As his parents had told him, in a very real way he was named after his grandfather, and the unusual way that he played the guitar.

Though not called Alfonso, Sterling's name had come from the proud family tradition that surrounded that little silver coin, whose high quality his parents felt made it seem like sterling, the purest type of silver, and thus a perfect choice as a name for their firstborn child. Though even his *abuelo* wasn't exactly sure where it had come from, the firmly held belief in the family was that this unique little silver coin had originated all the way back in the early days of California. According to the story, Alfonso's own great grandfather had proudly received and kept the coin, which his own father had passed down to him. Apparently, it had originally served as a part of a promissory note from the Spanish government, acknowledging the family's ownership of the land they had received from the Crown in the early days of the missions, *pueblos*, and *presidios* of Old California. While many of their fellow Mexican neighbors had lost their land as the Americans took over in later years, Sterling's great-great-great-grandfather had found a way to lay claim to his family's legacy—through the unique vintage of fine wines he had learned to produce on the family land, and, symbolically, through the silver coin he treasured and that he passed on to his children and grandchildren. Ever since, from one generation to the next, the coin had been passed down as a symbol of family pride, heritage, and legacy. It was something that Sterling was very proud of himself—that his name, Sterling, served as a reflection of his family's endurance and the tenacity of his people over all those many years.

Still, as the older Sterling stood there observing with nostalgia the scene from his youth, he couldn't help but sense a pang of regret that he had not paid closer attention when his grandfather was singing or telling stories or relating the events of his own youth and the traditions from generations gone by. And then, as he was contemplating the scene, a remarkable thing happened. Finishing his song with a plaintive air of wistfulness and romance, Alfonso lay down his guitar and carefully stowed away the silver coin that still glowed warmly in the light of the fire. Sitting down and calling his children and grandchildren to lean in closer, Alfonso began to speak.

"Sánchez." The singular word and name emerged from Alfonso's vigorous throat with solemn authority. "Sánchez is a name, but it is also a story. It is a sign of where our family comes from. It is our legacy." Sterling marvelled as he took in his grandfather's words, elated at the chance to hear once more a story he felt as though he had forgotten and yet had always been deeply a part of him.

"Any name has a history," Alfonso insisted, "but our history is not just any history." Continuing to speak, Alfonso began to outline the story of the family's early settlement and later trials and triumphs in Northern California.

"In our family, we trace our origins back to some of the first Mexican settlers of California. At the time, in the late 1700s, Mexico was still part of Spain, and the Spanish were convinced that this area where we now live was in danger. The British, the French, even the Russians, all had an eye on this place, and so the Spanish knew they needed to do something to keep the intruders out. And that's where we come in. One of your ancestors from many generations ago came as part of the *presidios*—the military bases the Spanish set up along the coast so they could reinforce their claims."

"What many don't remember," Alfonso continued, emphasizing with gravity the words he chose, "is that this land wasn't vacant. There were people here before our family arrived, and in fact they are part of our family, too."

Puzzled, the older Sterling leaned in to hear his grandfather's words more clearly, smiling knowingly as he noticed his younger self's eyelids drooping as the story continued.

"When the soldiers, the missionaries, and the other settlers first arrived, of course they didn't find an empty land. There were people here. There were tribes with their own customs and traditions that had been here for countless generations. And they were truly remarkable. They had learned how to cultivate the land in a way that was sustainable in the long-term. They fished from the rivers, they wove beautiful baskets and other wares with great artistry, they discerned how to care for the forests so that they could prevent devastating forest fires, and they even learned how to supplement their diet with ground acorns! Some of these folks welcomed the people from Mexico, and others resisted, and sadly many died in the process. I'm not proud of what many of the soldiers and the others did to the Indians, but I also know that others carried themselves with honor, and found a way to coexist and try to help the Indians as best they could."

"What's amazing about our family's story," Alfonso added, "is that we actually come from both the Mexican and the Native American lines. When our ancestor arrived from Mexico, not long afterward he met and fell in love with a girl who was living at the mission and had been separated from her family. They married and started a family, and their children were some of the original *californios*, the first people, after the Native Americans, to call this land of California home."

Sterling had heard the family stories many times growing up, and knew quite a lot of the history of his home state from his own studies. Proud to be part of the legacy of those who had first come to California from colonial Mexico, Sterling knew that his ancestors had not led easy lives, either under Spain or Mexico, and certainly not as part of the United States. Originally claiming the territory now encompassed by California and the southwest of the United States as far back as the early 1500s, Spain had come to refer to the territory as "California" by an amusing coincidence of history. As it turned out, many of the early Spanish conquerors had grown up in Spain familiar with a tale, popular at the time, of a mythical island paradise called Califia. Encountering the northwestern regions that stretched beyond central Mexico and that bordered the Pacific ocean, the early explorers christened the place "California," and the name stuck, though the land lay largely unexplored for centuries. Spain had sent a few initial exploratory expeditions, both by land and by sea, but encountered little in the way of land or resources that it considered worth the time and effort of colonization. In fact, several expeditions sailed right past the incalculably valuable natural harbor of San Francisco Bay without even noticing it, due to its famed fog.

With little reason to invest further, Spain's claim to the area largely remained one in name only until the 1700s, when word of growing incursions into the area by rival empires, among them even the Russians, reached the seat of colonial power in Mexico City. In order to respond to this threat, the colonial government realized it would need people on the ground to solidify its claim; it would need to settle and populate the region, ideally with many families from Mexico, but certainly with enough settlers, missionaries, and soldiers to convert and pacify the local Indian population, and secure a plausible claim to controlling the territory. It was a necessary task, and yet one that did not prove all that attractive to prospective colonists in Mexico. The journey many thousands of miles north was an arduous one, and the dangers and hardships of life on the margins of civilization as they knew it doubtless seemed unattractive at best to many potential recruits for the northward expeditions.

Sterling knew from the classes he had taken on California history that, without a doubt, the individuals who took on the task of exploring, missionizing, and settling California (or Alta California, as they would have called it) were, out of necessity, people of extraordinary determination. Making their way north in several expeditions, by the last few decades of the 1700s they had founded a series of religious missions, military fortifications, and towns that would form the nucleus of the Spanish presence in the land. Of course, for all their courage and bravado, these were flawed, imperfect people, and as Sterling knew, they had also been responsible for displacing, disrupting, and harming the native local peoples in various ways that led to these groups' rapid decline and impoverishment.

For that reason, it struck Sterling as incredibly remarkable, now that he was hearing his grandfather's story once more—and really for the first time—that his own family had lived personally the very tensions he knew had formed part of California's history. Surely, it must have been unimaginable for both of his ancestors—both the *presidio* soldier, and the young woman who became his bride—to negotiate the challenges and tensions of language, culture, empire, missions, and identity. And yet, here they all were, all these years later, the product of more than two centuries of cultural blending and change.

"What's amazing," Alfonso continued as Sterling processed all that was happening, "is that these ancestors never gave up, despite all that they faced. The soldier—his name was Luis—well, he soon learned after marrying his bride—her name was Tami—that his fellow soldiers were often unsympathetic, and even outrightly hostile, to his decision. They made life miserable for him, to the point that he could no longer serve in his role at the *presidio*, and he and Tami chose to make a go of it on their own, doing the best they could. With what little money they had, they purchased some land, and in the process, acquired this little silver coin."

Taking the coin out of his pocket, Alfonso held it in the air for his grandchildren to see, while his glance darted toward little Sterling, offering him a wink of recognition of the connection between the boy and the coin.

"Over time," Alfonso elaborated, "Luis and Tami worked and expanded their land, adding crops, raising livestock, and selling whatever they could to try to make a living and provide for their children. It was very hard work, and there were many setbacks, but with time, their *rancho* slowly prospered and they earned the respect of people throughout the *pueblo* of San Jose."

"Of course, as the years went by," Alfonso added, his expression clouding with a tinge of sadness, "new neighbors arrived who were not always as friendly. The anglo settlers came in larger and larger numbers. Many of them were good people, but others were out for land and were willing to do anything to get it. Sadly, that's how Luis and Tami lost most of their land. Either squatters, who came in and just took what they wanted, or the large landlords who took them to court and refused to accept the Spanish documents that they presented as evidence of their rightful ownership—either way, the end result was that Luis and Tami lost most of their land and all that they had worked so hard for over all those years.

"But . . ." Alfonso's taciturn expression suddenly shifted, as if a ray of light had shined suddenly into a dark cavern. "Even though Luis and Tami felt like they had lost just about everything, there was one small piece of their original land that no one seemed to be interested in. Off in a distant valley in the hills, the land seemed to be good for little of anything other than growing a few grapevines and fruit trees. And yet the silver coin they carried with them told them clearly that the land was theirs—that they had purchased it and that it was publicly recognized as their own."

Beaming with pride, Alfonso continued: "And so Luis and Tami built a new life for themselves and their family in the backcountry of the *pueblo* of San Jose. They built a home and carved out a farm and eventually found they could make a living with the grapes and the fruit that their land provided. And you know what, I'm convinced they're laughing with us from heaven now, because sure enough it turned out that they were sitting on a gold mine much richer than the ones the forty-niners looked for during the rush for gold in the mid-1800s, that made a very few people very rich in California and a whole lot of other people very, very poor.

"As it turned out," Alfonso went on, "the miners who came in 1849 and later years needed food and supplies and, when they were flush with cash, they also wanted wine, and so our family had the good fortune to be in the right place at the right time to provide them with those very things. Luis and Tami's children grew the vineyard and the fruit fields and found ways to can the fruit and get it to the miners and refine the techniques of wine cultivation that our family still follows. So even though it felt like they had lost everything in those years when they had to leave behind what they had built and start again, in time they were able to start a new life that brought them, and now all of us, so many blessings."

"In a way," Alfonso mused, holding up the silver coin once more, "it all really comes down to this little coin—this *sterling* coin—and what it represents: all the hard work and creativity and determination that has brought our family through rough times and helped us to build the farm and the vineyard that are still our livelihood today."

As Sterling listened intently to his grandfather's words, he knew instinctively that they were true. Against remarkable odds, his family, over many generations, had been part of establishing a culture that would live on in spite of many obstacles. It was this culture, this inheritance of a tradition deeply rooted in his people's presence in the land, that made Sterling proud to be who he was, a descendant of one of the original *californio* families, the Sánchez clan.

"Sánchez," Alfonso continued, as if in harmony with the ruminations of Sterling's memory, "is a name and a legacy to be proud of. Sánchez, our name, symbolizes the hard work and the pain and the joy and the perseverance that have all gone into making us who we are over all these many, many years. And it is all of you, the next generation, proud of who you are and where you come from, who will continue to pass on that legacy to your own children and grandchildren."

As Sterling took in his grandfather's words, weaving together the strands of family and local history that formed his heritage, his mind turned to the legacy of this proud past for the present. While aware of what his ancestors had lived through during the original Spanish colonial times, Sterling was also proud of what they had endured and successfully overcome in more recent years. It wasn't always easy being Latino and facing discrimination and misunderstanding, especially in a business world that often singled out and marginalized those who were different. Though he had many regrets, this was one thing Sterling could be proud of—something that he could say with confidence connected him deeply to who he really was.

Lost in thought, Sterling only realized when he looked up, back at his grandfather as he was finishing his story, that Chris had joined him. Startled, Sterling felt the need to ask where this was all going.

"Chris, I know physically where we are, but, seriously, where *are* we? How is all of this happening? What is happening to me?"

"Sterling, there's no need to fear," Chris responded with reassurance. "You're here because this is where you need to be right now."

"Hmm, well I guess I'll just have to trust you then."

"Yeah, not a bad idea," Chris said with a smile.

"This all seems pretty crazy, though," Sterling added with some trepidation.

Not missing a beat, Chris replied, "In time you'll see there's a method to my madness!"

With that the scene faded and shifted around them. The strains of Alfonso's music still ringing nostalgically in his ears, gradually the tone shifted, as the ringing turned high pitched and deafening. Perhaps it was the realization that he was still suspended within his demolished car, or that his blood pressure was spiraling downward due to the loss of blood—this horrific feeling of being trapped, with the thought of his own demise coming fast and furious. Sterling could feel the panic welling up inside his chest. With his heart racing out of control, he suddenly realized that he really had no other choice—he would have to surrender himself to this journey that Chris was offering him, whatever it really was and wherever it would lead. Feeling a sense of deep peace come over him, and hearing once more the strains of his grandfather's voice and the music of his guitar, Sterling felt confident that he could surrender to whatever lay ahead. Resting his thoughts for now, he knew that trusting and letting go would be the course he would need to take as long as this crazy journey lasted.

Chapter 3

Dark red grapes dangling above him, filling his hands, overflowing in buckets. It was the time of harvest in his family's vineyard, and Sterling recognized at once the unmistakable savor of juice in the air. He had no idea what this strange adventure was all about, but he was somehow glad that Chris had chosen to take him to such a happy part of his childhood. Each year harvest was a time when his family came together to work side by side; his sister, Mindy, and his parents, Rosita and José, and even his grandparents, uncles, aunts, close friends and neighbors. All gathered each year in the late summer when the countless rows of grapes they harvested were ready to be picked and taken for pressing.

Often, if the harvest were large enough, they would have help from Mexican farm worker families traveling through the area to find work. Sterling hadn't studied Spanish in school as a child, but he picked up quite a bit working alongside the families' children in the field as well as from his parents and grandparents in their ancestral tongue. His Spanish wasn't exactly elegant, but he'd learned enough to get his friends in trouble with their parents when he'd innocently pepper his phrases with liberal doses of colorful Mexican idioms and expressions.

As Sterling smiled, amused at his childhood cleverness, the scene gradually came into clearer view. He was standing at the top of the hill where his family's house sat overlooking the rolling expanse of vines extending in neat rows before him. He noticed that the workers were already starting their picking as the morning sun streamed out gradually from behind the foothills in the distance.

He even thought he could make out his parents in the background, heading toward the bins they would need to load onto the truck that would eventually pick up all that day's grapes. He called out to them and waved, but they kept on walking. Funny, he thought. He was about to call out to them again when, from seemingly out of nowhere, there was Chris again, standing at Sterling's side.

Smiling, Chris looked at Sterling and explained that this was no ordinary day in the vineyard. "Sterling," Chris said with gentle yet decisive care, "they can't hear you or see you."

"Really?" Sterling responded. "Is this a dream?"

"No," replied Chris. "It's very real. In fact, it's another day in your life that really happened many years ago. It's one of many places that we'll go together. But you'll have to just watch and observe. The time for making decisions and acting in each place has already come and gone. What you can do now is listen and see. Go, check it out."

Sterling wasn't sure what to make of Chris' instructions or really any of what was happening, but he knew it felt good to be back there—to be in a place that felt like home.

As he made his way reflectively down the driveway of the old house, considering what Chris had said and wondering just what day he'd arrived for, a scream suddenly pierced his eardrums, startling him and drawing his attention toward the small pond in the distance at the end of the row of vines.

Suddenly, instantly, he knew exactly what day it was. In his childhood years he'd known many families that passed through the area to help harvest the grapes each year, and he met and befriended many of the families' children. One family stood out in particular, though. The Domínguezes were one of several families that passed through each year, but Sterling had gotten to know several of their children, who were around his age, especially well. The friendship grew even deeper as the family eventually decided to put down roots in the valley and seek a way to make it their permanent home. This was not easy, as official visas were hard to come by. But little by little, coming and going back and forth to

Mexico, the family eventually received official permission to immigrate, and Sterling was thrilled when he found out they would be long-lasting neighbors and friends.

Sterling recalled that this day, the day that Chris had brought him back to, was right around the time the Domínguezes had permanently settled in the area. Two of the family's children, Ignacio and Leti, both a few grade levels above Sterling in school, were particularly close friends. The three of them were inseparable, working together in the fields, riding their bikes into town when they were able, and spending many an afternoon swimming and playing in the small pond located at the edge of the property.

That particular day had started out like countless others. The three friends had worked outside in the morning, took a break for lunch, and were playing and swimming in the pond in the afternoon. Sometimes they would be called back to work by their parents, and that's what happened that day. Sterling and Leti grudgingly assented to the orders and started making their way out of the water and back up the hill toward the fields. Ignacio was having none of it, though. The two friends called out to him, but he yelled that he'd be fine and would catch up with them soon. At the time, Sterling was a bit unsure about it, as Ignacio was not a strong swimmer. Still, his friend was just wading by the side of the pond and Sterling was sure he'd be fine.

Sterling had made his way back to the processing building, where the grapes were gathered for pressing, when he heard Leti's scream. Turning around instantaneously, Sterling knew instinctively what was happening. Leti had gone back to check on Ignancio and something was terribly wrong. Sterling raced with all the strength he could muster down the rows of vines and ripening grapes, straining to decipher through the rows of foliage what was happening at the pond, now seemingly miles beyond his reach.

Finally, Sterling reached the edge of the pond and took in the scene. Ignacio, instead of stepping out of the pond and walking around it to make his way back to the farm, had decided to try to swim across. He had made it about halfway before he realized how deep the water reached in the middle. No longer able to stand,

Ignancio was flailing and screaming for help, with Leti calling out as she tried to paddle out toward him. Instantly, Sterling knew what he had to do. Throwing off his shoes and outer clothing, he dove in and tore through the water toward his friend. Using all the skills he'd learned over many summers of swim lessons and time with the local swimming team, Sterling quickly reached Ignacio. Grabbing him under his arms and across his chest, Sterling pulled his friend toward the shore, meeting Leti halfway and enlisting her to help carry Ignacio to shore. By this time Sterling's own parents, along with Leti and Ignacio's and many of the other workers, had rushed to the shore to help.

However, no one was prepared for the scene that was about to play out before them. Carrying Ignacio as best he could onto solid ground, Sterling pulled his friend to safety, only to realize something was terribly wrong. Seeing Ignacio's mouth and eyes closed, several of those who had gathered around began to shout, calling out for someone to call an ambulance, which Leti ran back toward the house to do. With no time to think, much less to worry or panic, Sterling sprang into action, opening his friend's mouth to let some of the water out and then beginning the steps of CPR he had learned in training as a lifeguard. As Sterling tried to revive Ignacio, alternating between quick mouth breaths and chest compressions, deep down he also said a prayer, asking God to spare his friend and help him come back. As he continued the compressions, the young Sterling was just starting to feel the sting of tears welling up in his eyes as he prayed for a miracle, when suddenly he looked up and saw one of the paramedics who had just arrived on the scene. Looking at Sterling with kindness that was palpable and moving, the man made his way toward him and told him firmly, "Young man, you're doing an excellent job. Now we're here to help." At exactly the same moment that Sterling heard the man's words enter his ears, he felt Ignacio's body jump beneath his hands as his friend stirred back to life before his eyes. Moved with gratitude, Sterling and the others came together to embrace Ignacio, holding him close and giving thanks that he had come back to life.

As the older Sterling watched, he sensed deeply once more the overwhelming thankfulness he and the others had experienced that day. And yet there was an added element of something Sterling found difficult to put into words. There, witnessing the scene again, Sterling had relived any number of profound emotions. But nothing could prepare him for the realization he had, looking up from his younger self's perspective, to see the paramedic walking toward him at what seemed like his most hopeless moment. Startled and yet filled with wonder, the older Sterling realized in that moment that the paramedic was none other than Chris. He had always known there was something strikingly familiar about his companion in this crazy journey they had set out on, but now he knew what it was. Somehow, in some mysterious way, Chris was a part of his life—a wise friend and someone he knew in a profound way would help lead him through to where he needed to go. Glancing over at Chris, he knew he didn't need to say a word. Perceiving his friend's broad smile as he gazed at the scene they were both watching, Sterling knew in a way beyond explanation that this was where he needed to be—that this was the path that would somehow lead him home.

Reflecting on the intensity of what had just happened, Sterling realized that this wasn't the first time he had reached out to help someone. Experiencing once more the scene with Ignacio reminded Sterling of what had by that point in his childhood become a habit of heart, stemming from his relationship with his younger sister, Mindy. As someone with Down Syndrome, Mindy had special gifts that weren't always recognized or appreciated, especially by classmates in school. Sterling had grown up loving his sister and defending her when classmates would harass or bully her. More than that, though, what stood out for Sterling about his sister was just how amazing she was. Even more than his anger at the other kids for their cruelty, he felt genuinely sorry for them for missing out on a truly great person. Mindy had a love of life and a contagious ability to laugh that never ceased to amaze him. He loved his sister dearly and now, looking back on it, he realized it was her presence in his life that made him more sensitive and aware of the needs of others than most of his peers. No doubt, he thought, it was Mindy who had planted the seeds of the kind of attentiveness and awareness that had enabled him to do what he did that day in pulling Ignacio out of the water.

Remembering his sister and her role in his childhood touched Sterling deeply, but at the same time reminded him again that he was no longer a child. He felt a pang of sadness as he thought about how things had developed later. Going off to college and then making it big, eventually Mindy played less and less of a role in Sterling's life. He still saw her once in a while during his increasingly infrequent visits home, or said "hi" briefly over the phone, but they'd grown apart and, standing there, taking in the scene of that long-ago day, Sterling knew deep down that the responsibility was his. And he didn't like it. Surely, he thought, he needed to do better. *Where is Chris?* he wondered. It was time to move on to hopefully a happier, less burdensome memory.

Chapter 4

MAKING HIS WAY BACK slowly toward the main house, Sterling turned his gaze briefly back toward the water where the scene with Ignacio had played out. As he did, suddenly Chris was there with him again.

"Well, you certainly know how to make an entrance!" Sterling quipped sarcastically.

"Come on. Where's your sense of humor, Ster?" Chris responded. "And, by the way, do you remember when people stopped calling you by your nickname?"

"Hmm . . . no, not really," Sterling replied.

"Perhaps the next place we need to visit, then, is that moment," Chris added with a touch of irony in his voice.

"I'm thinking I'd better go along with this, eh?" Sterling added with a smile.

"Now that's the spirit!" Chris laughed.

Slowly, before Sterling realized fully what was happening, the scene began to change around them. The gentle ripples in the lake's water gradually lightened in color and the familiar surroundings of the countryside transformed little by little into an equally recognizable, but different, scene. Before long, Sterling knew exactly where he was. Unmistakably, it was his high school swimming pool. The smell of chlorine wafted through the air as lapping wavelets splashed over the sides of the pool in the wake of swimmers making their way back and forth in the constant repetition that was the daily practice Sterling and his teammates submitted themselves to for many years of their childhood and adolescence. Although he was tall and lean, Sterling didn't have it easy at first as a swimmer. He had to work hard at his technique in his adolescent years, but by college he remembered feeling like he could coast a bit more—like he was entitled to the awards and accolades, including the college scholarship, that eventually came his way.

As Sterling took in the sights and sounds of the pool and the many swimmers, gradually the scene changed subtly, shifting from the familiar trappings of daily practice to the rigors of an important swim meet at the same pool. Taking in the scene, Sterling noticed that the pool was now empty and that many of the swimmers on the teams participating in the meet were gathered toward the far end where the starting blocks were located. More than just eight individuals for the eight lanes demarcated by the lines of bobbing markers stretched across the sky-blue water, Sterling knew right away that the race he was about to watch was not an individual event but a relay. Behind each of the eight blocks, four swimmers from the different participating teams gathered, stretching, breathing in out out with focused concentration, and otherwise gathering themselves in mental and physical preparation for the important race—the very last and the most determinative of the meet—to begin. Looking out across the sunlit water, Sterling noticed right away his high school teammates gathered behind the block for lane four. As the designated place for the relay team with the fastest time going into the event, he and his teammates enjoyed a privileged position in the pool that would hopefully provide them just the edge they needed to out-touch the other teams in the battle of fractions of a second at the end of the race.

Focusing more clearly on the deck area behind the block, Sterling could discern the faces of his three teammates, each seemingly focused on the race ahead and finishing the last adjustments to their goggles and swim caps as they prepared to race. And yet, Sterling thought, isn't someone missing? Where is the fourth person? Who was anchoring the relay? Casting his gaze around the pool area, Sterling struggled to discern who it could have been that was so late to the blocks that day. Didn't they know that they needed to be there, Sterling thought to himself. Where was their commitment to the team and to the relay?

Then, just as his view turned toward the stands on the opposite side of the pool, Sterling caught sight of the answer to his queries. There, directly across the pool from where the older Sterling was sitting, was the unmistakable sight of his younger self splayed comfortably across the uppermost bench of the stands. With sunglasses donned, fully clothed in his sweatsuit, and, it seemed, blithely unaware of anything other than the pizza he was chomping down as he laughed with a group of friends, the younger Sterling seemed anything but focused in on the important race about to get underway in the pool below.

The older Sterling could hardly believe it. This was clearly an important meet, judging by the teams gathered to compete and what he remembered about how competitively each group vied for the coveted state title each year. Struggling to grasp what was happening, the older Sterling, undetected by anyone gathered at the meet, made his way along the deck at the side of the pool, working his way among the crowd of judges and officials toward the blocks and, he was determined, his younger self, if not to talk some sense into him then at least to try to understand what he might have been thinking.

Weaving in and out among the swimmers gathered behind the blocks, the older Sterling felt almost ashamed to pass by his teammates in lane four. Leaving plenty of space between them and him, even though he knew they could neither see nor hear him, Sterling was about to pass by them when he overheard a snippet of their conversation that stopped him dead in his tracks.

"Oh yeah," one teammate said, with a mixture of sarcasm and seeming exhaustion, "Good old Ster's not here, yet again."

"I seriously cannot believe he's pulling this again on us," another teammate chimed in. "I mean, really, who the hell does he think he is? Does he think the world just revolves around him, or that he can do whatever pleases? This is really getting old."

"Yup," the third member of the relay added with a nod and a sigh, "we've all talked with him and it seems like there's just no way to get through to him. He's pulled this several times now and it's really way out of bounds. I just hope he can pull out the win again this one last time. We've been really lucky these past few meets, but I'm scared that it might not be so easy today."

Casting his eyes down in disappointment with himself, the older Sterling walked away from the conversation, not wanting to hear any more of the well-deserved scorn he knew his teammates would continue to direct his way. More determined than ever now to get to the bottom of what his younger self could possibly have been thinking, Sterling continued to wind his way among the swimmers and officials behind the blocks, slowly progressing toward the opposite stands, where he could see his younger self chugging down a large bottle of soda as he continued to laugh and mingle with his companions at the top of the stands.

Focusing in all the more determinedly on reaching his younger self as he walked toward the stands, Sterling was surprised when the familiar whistle signaling the start of the race pierced his ears and he heard the announcer inform the fans and supporters of the team names and lane numbers. Realizing he wouldn't have time to make it all the way to the top of the stands before the race began, Sterling settled into a seat near the poolside where he could take in both the race about to get underway and the spectacle of his younger self's continued obliviousness.

With the familiar tension in the air and the sound of the words "Swimmers, take your mark" spoken tersely over the public address system, the pool area quieted as the first person in each relay took his stance on the block. Then, with the speed of a bullet, the noise of the starter's gun pierced the air and the swimmers were off. The race had begun, and already it was a very close one. Sterling watched as his first teammate navigated the water with impressive alacrity, plying the waves stirred up by the other swimmers with a clean, crisp freestyle that carried his body gracefully through the water. Before it seemed possible, Sterling's next team-mate was already in the water, bearing down on the competitor in lane five who had managed to gain a slight lead coming off the starting blocks. Soon the second teammate likewise had powered his way to the wall, and the third swimmer was flying through the air, diving headlong into his lane and forging his way just slightly ahead of the competition in lane five.

Almost forgetting his vendetta against his younger self, the older Sterling had immersed himself in the adrenaline of the mo-ment, cheering on his teammates and hoping against hope they would be able to pull off the win. Then, glancing up behind him, Sterling struggled to believe what he was seeing. There, distracted in conversation with several young ladies from the girls' team, the younger Sterling continued to laugh hysterically, prone on the bench with his legs crossed, arms positioned comfortably behind his head, and sunglasses still in place. And then, just when the older Sterling thought he was literally going to jump three benches at a time up to the top of the seats to shake some sense into his younger self, one of the young ladies, turning toward the unfolding events below in the pool, tapped Sterling on the shoulder with a quizzical expression.

Turning his head and doffing his sunglasses, the younger Sterling slowly sat up and mouthed a colorful expression the older Sterling could make out with a combination of anger and bemused clarity. For what must have been no more than a second but which seemed like an eternity, the younger Sterling sat there at the top of the stands with his mouth gaping, stunned at the realization of where he currently was and where he needed to be. And then, as if by some stunning alchemy, his body, his expression, and his location transformed instantaneously. Before the older Sterling could fully grasp what was happening, his younger self had shed the sweatsuit he had been wearing over his swimsuit and was bounding down the stairs of the bleachers, two or more at a time. Sprinting toward the blocks, with no time to gather his goggles or cap, the younger Sterling leaped into position just as his teammate was nearing the wall. With just enough time to judge the distance of the other swimmer's reach, the young Sterling rocketed off the block, streamlining through the air and into the water. Beating through the roiling waves like he never had before, the young Sterling swam with a determination that the older Sterling, even in his anger with his younger self, had to admit was impressive. Making the turn and coming back toward the finish line, the older Sterling knew his younger self could not see a thing without the goggles he always wore. This was a moment of pure adrenaline. There was no way around it; either Sterling would pull it off or he wouldn't. It really came down to how much energy he had left to be able to touch out his competitor in lane five.

As the swimmers neared the wall, the older Sterling could not breathe. It was entirely too much to even begin to take in. The stakes were so incredibly high, and there was no possible way to know who was ahead. Sterling and his rival in lane five were that close. As if in slow motion, the competitors bore into the last second of the race, each hammering his arm in the furthest extension possible into the wall and the automatic timing system embedded inside. For a moment, it seemed that time had stopped, that the world had paused, suspended in midair as the roar of the crowd echoed around the pool complex. After what was probably no more than one second but seemed to the older Sterling like hours, he found the strength to glance up to the scoreboard where the official times were displayed.

It was impossible, and yet it was what the clock read out. By one one-hundredth of a second, lane four had touched out lane five. Sterling's team had won. The relay that, up until the final moments of the race, had consisted of only three swimmers, had somehow pulled out the win. It was amazing. It was miraculous. It was also just plain crazy. As he struggled to take in the enormity of what had happened, the older Sterling glanced across the water and looked on with wonder as he viewed his younger self seemingly leap out of the water, his fist raised in a triumphant sign of victory, his teammates hastening to his side, as the glory of the moment rushed in for all to absorb.

Closing his eyes in disbelief, the older Sterling took in the roar of the crowd and marvelled at both the unflinching bravado and the sheer stupidity of his younger self. Still reveling in the moment, he opened his eyes again, but now to a transformed space at the same pool. Looking around, Sterling realized that he was once again back in his original position sitting in the stands above the pool during swim practice, though now he noticed that Chris was there next to him.

"A place you know well, I see," Chris said knowingly.

"You bet," Sterling exclaimed. "This was where the magic happened. Did you see what just went down at that meet?! I rocked the place!"

"Yes, you most certainly did," Chris responded. "You were the best. All the records, all the accolades. You were the greatest swimmer to pass through this school and you knew it."

"Well, just look at the record boards, man," Sterling boasted. "Not too many of mine have fallen, even though it's been quite a few years now."

"You bet," Chris acknowledged. "In fact, this day that we've come back to was one of your greatest."

"Really?" Sterling replied.

"Yup," Chris added. "Just look over there to the other side of the bleachers and you'll remember."

Sterling glanced toward the pool and felt a startling sense of recognition as he took in the scene. There he was, his seventeen-year-old self, jumping out of the pool as practice ended and making his way over to a gruff, serious-looking middle-aged man in shorts and a clean, bright shirt with the words "Ocean Pacific University" printed on the lapel. Sterling knew instantly what this moment was, and Chris could sense it.

"Feel free, Sterling," Chris chimed in, reading Sterling's mind. "Remember, they can't see or hear us. Go over and listen in if you'd like." Sterling made his way quickly over to the scene of the conversation as it got underway, though not without first chuckling as he saw his younger self make a little detour on his way to the coach.

Already at that time in high school, Sterling had styled himself a popular man-about-campus, and didn't miss any chances to make an impression. As he made his way toward the coach, he saw a group of cheerleaders on the side of the pool getting ready to support the team in the meet that was about to start. Veering over toward them, the younger Sterling yelled over to the young ladies, asking them if they were there to see him, and letting them know they were sure to be impressed. Unsure what to make of him, the cheerleaders smiled nervously, but Sterling didn't seem bothered. In any case, he knew without a doubt that they were there for him, even as he made his way toward a scene that his older self, now taking in the whole scene, knew would change his life forever. Now close to the conversation that was starting to develop, the older Sterling listened in . . .

". . . and that's just the beginning, Sterling. You're already an excellent athlete, but you can do even better." It was Bob Carson, head coach of the Ocean Pacific men's and women's swim teams and one of the most respected mentors in the sport. The older Sterling marveled at the fact that this remarkable coach had driven all that way to visit his younger self. It really was an honor, now that he thought about it.

"Yeah, I guess you're right. Swimming's always just kind of come naturally to me," the younger Sterling quipped to Carson. "I work hard but honestly it's the chance to trounce the competition that I really enjoy."

"Interesting," Carson replied, "Competition and drive are important. Having worthy opponents can make athletes even better than they ever thought they could be. But it's gotta be balanced with sportsmanship, too. You don't get to the very top unless you have some sense of the bigger picture."

"Sure," Sterling responded, assenting to Bob's advice without much reflection. "You know, though, I'm not sure you're going to find anyone much faster than me among this year's recruits. I'm pretty much the best."

"You are very talented, Sterling," Bob replied, ignoring for now the shallowness of Sterling's comment. "And there's a lot that we can teach you at Ocean Pacific, if you're up for the challenge."

"You bet, man," Sterling said. "So it's a done deal, then?"

"Yes, Sterling," Bob responded, "We're prepared to offer you a full-tuition swimming scholarship to Ocean Pacific. There are many privileges that go along with that, as well as responsibilities. Are you ready to take those on?"

"Don't sweat it, dude," Sterling replied with a smirk. "I'm your man."

"Well, I look forward to working with you, Sterling," Bob said in reply. "You have the kind of potential that matches your name: Sterling."

"Exactly," Sterling shouted out as he ran toward the locker room. "It's time to use my full name if I'm going to be Ocean Pacific's next big star!"

With that the young Sterling disappeared into the locker room, leaving the older Sterling both to laugh at the bravado of his young self and to sense just a tinge of discomfort. As he looked back from his old self to Bob's face he saw the coach roll his eyes and shake his head. "Yeah," thought Sterling, "not exactly the moment of my greatest humility."

Sterling turned toward Chris, still sitting in the stands and now wearing a knowing grin on his face, "Come on, Sterling," Chris motioned to him. "It's time to pay Ocean Pacific's newest star a visit."

"Oh boy," Sterling replied with a mixture of amusement and dread.

"Oh yeah" was Chris' knowing reply.

Chapter 5

5:30 AM AND IT was time to get up. Sterling felt a sense of recognition as the scene began to take shape around him. He and Chris had stumbled back into yet another distant memory, this one from the early days of Sterling's athletic and academic career at Ocean Pacific. As Sterling took in the scene, he recognized right away the contours of his old dorm room on campus. Located on an upper floor, his room looked out over the picturesque lawns and pathways of the university grounds, slowly starting to awaken.

Well, some were waking. In the room that he shared with three roommates, all of them fellow swimming teammates, everyone was stirring—beginning the daily ritual of preparation for practice, which started promptly at 6:00 AM each day. Everyone, that is, except Ocean Pacific's star freshman swimmer, Sterling. As his teammates threw their suits and towels in their backpacks and started heading out, one of them, Justin, called back to Sterling.

"Hey man, you're going to miss practice again! You know what coach said. Any more like that and you'll be off the team."

"Whatever" was the only response Sterling could muster as he rolled over in bed, pulling the covers above his head and trying to forget about the throbbing headache seeming to rend his skull in two. It hurt his forehead just to have the sheet touch it. Yes, yet another hangover after yet another night of drinking and partying. To Sterling, college was supposed to be something to enjoy and he wasn't about to miss out on any of it.

"Well, I'm not covering for you this time," Jason called out as he left. "You better hope that coach gives you another chance or you're done."

Jason really was a good friend, the older Sterling thought as he took in the scene. For all his insistence, Sterling realized (perhaps for the first time) that his friend really had been looking out for him. And, he had to admit, his younger self probably could have benefited from some of that care and concern if he'd been more open to it. Sure, all the parties, all the late nights were great, but maybe it wouldn't have killed him to get up that day. Or, better yet, to have gotten back at a reasonable time the night before. But the booze had been flowing and the female partiers just too hot to walk away from! The ladies expected him to perform for them and so he did. He could *never* let them down, and he certainly would *never* say "no" to a sure thing! But now, yet again, he was paying the consequence of his late night follies.

"Yup, exactly," Chris interjected, smiling.

"Wait a minute—how'd you know what I was thinking?" the older Sterling replied with astonishment.

"No more internal monologue here," Chris said with a smirk. "I'm here to help you and I'm going to need all the advantages I can get to try and understand how that brain of yours could be both so sharp and so foolish at the same time."

"Great," Sterling added with a sigh. "Guess I probably deserve that."

"Just think of it as a way that I can help you help yourself, Sterling," Chris replied.

"Well, how about helping me learn the trick, so I can read people's minds, too?" Sterling added with amusement. "It would definitely come in handy with my business dealings!"

"Maybe someday, Sterling, but first you've got to learn to know your own mind, your own self," Chris responded. "The rest will follow."

"If you say so," Sterling countered with playful skepticism.

"You know, now that you mention it, Sterling, maybe it would be good for you to see a little bit of things from a different perspective," Chris added. "While you were passed out here in the bed, let's look at what was happening at the practice you were supposed to be at. You won't be able to read minds, but I don't think it'll take much effort for you to get a read on the situation."

"Ah, now this could be interesting," Sterling replied.

"Oh, I think so," Chris said, nodding in agreement.

As Chris' words registered in Sterling's mind, the scene suddenly began to change rapidly around him. From the comforts of his college dorm room, he suddenly noticed a very different but equally familiar scene unfold around him. It was the unmistakable odor of chlorine and the sound of feet and hands slicing through water that told Sterling without a doubt that he was at swim practice. Not just any swim practice, though. This was the large aquatic center that, for awhile at least, had become Sterling's second home in college. Featuring eight lanes of full Olympic-size competition and training space, the pool was state of the art—fully equipped and designed to facilitate the rise of great athletes for the school, and, ideally, for the nation.

As advanced as the facilities were, even more crucial to the athletic aspirations of the university and its athletes were the coaches and trainers who helped make real swimmers out of the rough-and-tumble high school kids who made their way to the pool decks each fall. Standing out among these leaders was the team's head coach, Bob Carson. Bob was an outstanding mentor and guide to the young people who swam for him. Tough and demanding, Bob was respected by his swimmers and beloved as well for the genuine care he showed for each of them. His aspiration was to make them into champions, but helping them grow as young men and women with outstanding character was an equally crucial facet of what he saw as his vocation to serve young people.

Taking on the responsibility of coaching and mentoring his very selective, elite team of swimmers was a task Bob took with utmost seriousness. You didn't swim for Bob unless you were the very best of the best, and you meant business. Selecting who would be invited to the team was a very serious task, and Bob didn't like taking risks. And yet, every once in a while an athlete would come along that just might be worth the gamble. Bob knew in these situations there were no guarantees, and yet sometimes the natural talent a swimmer might bring simply stood out and compelled him to take the chance.

Such was the case, as his younger self had intuited, for Sterling. Just as much as Bob knew it, Sterling too sensed deep down that he had a gift. For Bob, it was a remarkable ability to behold—one that only came along once in a very great while. And so, despite the reservations he had over Sterling's immaturity, over the numerous stories Sterling's high school coaches and teachers had shared about his ego, Bob knew that he had to at least give it a shot. Who knows—perhaps this young man was destined to achieve something great as a swimmer.

It was with that knowledge of Sterling's potential, as well as his personal failings, that Bob clinched his jaw and heaved a deep sigh as Sterling's friend Jason stuck his head into Bob's office on the way to the locker room that morning to report that Sterling was running late. Once again, in what was becoming a distressing pattern, Sterling was late for practice. Excuses and half-hearted apologies always abounded, but this time Bob knew things had to be different. His other swimmers were starting to take note, and team morale was suffering. The team's star swimmer was holding back the potential of his teammates and setting a poor example. As regrettable and difficult as it was going to be, Bob knew he had to seize the bull by his horns and take action. He'd gambled and taken a risk, and alas it seemed that, at least for now, he'd lost.

Chapter 6

As Bob was sadly, yet inevitably, coming to his conclusion about Sterling's place on the team, Sterling himself (in his younger manifestation, that is) was making his way erratically toward the pool. Stumbling down the stairs of his dorm in his shorts and sandals, he struggled into a worn-out T-shirt and raced across the main quad toward the large athletic complex on the other side of campus, with its imposing group of athletic stadiums, fields, and fatefully that day, the Olympic-sized competitive aquatic complex. The pool where the swim team practiced daily was located outside, to take best advantage of the sun and warmth of the southern California climate.

Making his way toward the pool, Sterling could distinguish the familiar sight of his teammates making their way back and forth through the water, thinking that he might just have made it in time to escape Coach Bob's notice. Sterling was startled when Bob appeared seemingly out of nowhere, blocking his entrance to the gate, and therefore to a surreptitious, undetected entrance into the pool. Frustrated in his plans, and now that he was caught, Sterling, tried to contemplate the next best option. Thinking that playing for sympathy might be his best shot, Sterling begged Bob's forgiveness.

"Bob, my man," Sterling began with eyes cast down. "You wouldn't believe it. I lost track of time and totally forgot about practice. Man, this will never happen again."

Sad, yet steeled in his determination, Bob replied firmly to Sterling. "You know, Sterling, you're absolutely right. This will never happen again. The reason why is that you're never going to set foot in this pool again. You're off the team. You're done."

"What?!" Sterling exclaimed in reply. "You can't do that to me, dude. I'm your best swimmer by far. You all are nothing without me!"

"Sterling, you may have talent. But in swimming (and, you know, in life too), it takes more than that to succeed. You've gotta have some discipline and self-control, and you've shown me nothing but the exact opposite of both those things ever since you joined this team. Maybe someday you'll be able to put together those things, find a way to use your talents well. But I can tell you that it won't be today, and it won't ever again be on this swim team."

"But, Bob," Sterling protested. "What am I going to do? How am I going to pay for college if I lose my scholarship?"

"You know, Sterling," Bob replied, "I'm usually a pretty patient guy, and I've given you a lot of chances. But the fact is you messed up. You're going to lose your scholarship and I have no idea what you'll do to pay for your tuition. Frankly, it's not my problem anymore. Maybe, just maybe, you'll learn a lesson through all of this and find your way."

"Lesson? What lesson?" was all Sterling could think to say in response. "How can I learn anything if I can't even pay for school?"

"Sterling, I've got swimmers and a practice to get back to," Bob responded, turning back toward the gate to the pool. "I wish you luck. You're not a bad kid. You just have a lot to learn. You may not agree now, but someday you'll thank me. Just wait and see."

With that Bob turned his back and walked quickly away, leaving the young Sterling speechless for one of the rare moments in his life. As his younger self stood there still trying to take it all in, the older Sterling and Chris watched the scene from a short distance. To the older Sterling, it was a surreal moment. Here he was, he thought to himself, reliving the mistakes of his early years, and yet somehow knowing now, with a little more distance and perspective, that things weren't quite the way he used to remember them. In previous times, in the rare moments when he'd thought back on episodes like the final confrontation with Bob, it was with resentment and self-righteousness. He'd been the one wronged. Bob had been unfair to him. His talents and potential on the team were never properly appreciated.

There was a whole lot of story there, and yet somehow, looking back on it now from this utterly unique vantage point, Sterling thought that just maybe Bob had been right. After all, it wasn't Bob's fault that he'd dedicated more time to frat parties than to getting proper rest. It wasn't Bob's fault that he'd mostly relinquished the leadership role on the team that could easily have been his. In any event, Sterling could see that Bob had been right about one thing for sure: without his decision to kick him off the team, Sterling probably would never have had the motivation, drive, or sheer ambition that it took to start out in his next venture. Sterling smiled as he thought of it.

As Sterling beamed with an amusement mildly tinged with the regret he'd come to feel over the events he had just relived, Chris too smiled knowingly. Discerning Sterling's thoughts, Chris didn't hesitate to interject.

"Sterling," Chris whispered with a smile. "I do think Bob was correct. But he just had no clue the fun you were going to have proving him right!"

With that both Chris and Sterling burst out laughing—a welcome relief for Sterling from the seriousness of looking back and taking stock on his life.

"Yeah," Sterling responded. "He had no idea!"

Suddenly, as Sterling chuckled over the irony of the situation, the scene began to change around him. Little by little the smell of chlorine and the sound of swimmers traveling back and forth in the pool faded as a new scene came into view. It was a place readily familiar to Sterling and it didn't take long for him to know where he was.

As Sterling's vision came back into focus, he looked around the room that he had come to know so well following his expulsion from the room he had shared with his teammates. Located on the ground floor of the house belonging to Ocean Pacific's most infamous men's fraternity, he took in the familiar smell of beer and liquor, peppered with the stench of cigar smoke, and the sight of his fraternity brothers gathered in a meeting. Even more surprising, he soon realized exactly the occasion in the fraternity's storied history that Chris had helped him to stumble back on.

Sterling's dismissal from the team had happened in early November of his freshman year, and he remembered well what had followed after. Turning from his now-defunct scholarship to a number of high-interest student loans, throwing himself headlong into the party scene, and abandoning any pretense of responsibility, Sterling had embraced the hedonism of frat life at its best (or, perhaps, worst). Since he was no longer burdened with the responsibilities of the team, Sterling's fraternity elders had assigned him more work in the house. Specifically, it was the new pledge's task to assist in the procurement of alcohol for each weekend's events. Since Sterling was still under twenty-one at this point, the new task presented something of a challenge. Then again, the older Sterling reminisced, when he set his mind to it there were few challenges that could get in his way.

Sterling's first attempt at procurement was not exactly what he would have called a success. Finding himself with the responsibility to provide alcohol for the next weekend's parties, Sterling knew he had to come up with a plan. Not knowing where to start, he figured he would try what he had heard worked for a number of other underage partiers on campus. According to urban legend, one of the local liquor stores was known to be a place where fake IDs got nothing more than a passing glance, and so constituted an ideal spot to procure libations for parties. Thinking this the ideal solution, Sterling made his way to the store on a Friday afternoon, confident his mature good looks and winning swagger would convince even a more skeptical store employee that he could be trusted with whatever liquor he managed to pay for.

Strolling into the store, Sterling grabbed a cart and made his way through the aisles, tossing in several cases of beer, wine, and various bottles of hard liquor—all key elements of a successful frat house event. Making his way to the cash register, Sterling felt a stirring of excitement that he would be able to pull this off. Probably, he thought, he wouldn't even need to show ID. The young lady behind the counter would fall victim to his charms and forget even the possibility of asking his age.

As it turned out, that wasn't exactly the way things unfolded. Arriving finally at the register, Sterling turned his gaze beguilingly up toward the young woman, expectantly hoping for a wink and a smile in return, only to be shocked to look up in time to see her eyes roll and to hear her sigh audibly as she snapped, "ID, please."

Frozen in place, Sterling had no idea what to do. He didn't have his fake ID with him, and even if he did, it sure didn't seem like this girl was going to overlook its obvious inauthenticity. And yet he had to get something for the guys back at the frat house—he couldn't come back empty-handed. And so he did the only thing that came to mind—he grabbed the nearest carton of beer cans in his cart and he ran *fast*. Bolting out the door, he barely had time to distinguish the cashier's words as she screamed "*Thief!*" and something about "the cops!" Sterling knew that whatever it was, it wasn't good, and so he just ran, and ran, and ran some more. Weaving in and out of yards, fences, and cars in the neighborhood on the way back to campus, he didn't stop till he crashed through the back door of the frat house, practically tumbling down the stairs to the basement and throwing the beer off into the back corner. Panting for air, he marveled that he had made it without getting caught, and yet he knew that even he wasn't up to this kind of adventure every week. He would need to come up with a new plan, and before long he stumbled on one that he was convinced would work perfectly.

As fate would have it, one week not long after his departure from the team, Sterling found himself at the beginning of the week without a reliable buyer for the coming weekend's house event. In the weeks since his shoplifting extravaganza, he had developed a temporary new strategy, working through the fraternity's network of alumni and friends to find someone willing to take a trip to a different local liquor store to pick up supplies for the coming weekend's celebrations. However, this week no offers were forthcoming as a result of a recent crackdown by the administration. Over-twenty-one buyers were warned to beware: the school's leadership was on to them and would prosecute them if they were caught. To say the least, this had a notable chilling effect on Sterling's normally game list of volunteers. The dilemma was clear: no one was willing to buy, and yet the very reputation and perhaps ongoing social credibility of his fraternity was on the line. And it all was about to fall on him. If Sterling didn't act, chances were that he would take the fall and perhaps even lose his membership in the fraternity.

One dismissal was bad enough, the young Sterling had thought. He wasn't about to let some stuffy administrators risk his status in another group that meant a lot to him, not to mention take away the fun and excitement he was convinced was the real reason for him to be in college anyway. And then Sterling had an idea. He was surprised it hadn't occurred to him earlier. It was a simple plan, and yet so brilliant. He had all that he needed right there in front of him.

As it turns out, Sterling knew a thing or two about liquor. Having grown up surrounded by a vineyard and in a family in the winemaking business, he knew exactly what it took to produce fine-quality alcohol. Moreover, he had also taken a few unofficial lessons from some of the workers who lived near the farm, who made their own homemade beer, moonshine, and other brews. It was so simple. Sterling realized that all he had to do was gather together a few supplies, set up shop down in the fraternity's basement, and get to work. In no time, there would be an ample supply of spirits that would make his fraternity the envy of all the other houses on the block. Now it was just a matter of recruiting a few volunteers, gathering the supplies, and starting up what he sensed was going to be a brilliant new venture.

Setting the plan in motion, Sterling knew just what to do. It would be bold and a little risky, but he was sure he could pull it off. All he had to do was skip class that day, drive quickly back up to Northern California to the family vineyard, and spirit away a few necessities—empty bottles, hoses, kettles, some grains, and a few other items he knew some of the workers kept on the grounds. Throwing a few items for the road into his backpack, Sterling was off, charging frenetically up US Highway 101 back toward the Bay Area.

Night had already set in by the time Sterling pulled into the narrow road off the highway leading up to his family's property. Judging from the parking lot that the workers had all gone home for the night, he knew it was safe to drive furtively past the main house and park unnoticed in the back of one of the auxiliary storage barns at the edge of the vineyard. Letting himself in, Sterling was pleased to find just the supplies he needed, and was back on the road in no time.

It was probably not the best idea, Sterling thought, but he was so excited to get his new operation underway that he decided to pull an all-nighter and drive all the way back to school before morning. It was kind of crazy, Sterling knew, but on the other hand, this way he could skip class again and get started right away setting up the apparatus. Cranking up the music and pounding back a few energy drinks, Sterling was wired and ready to go, and by the time he reached L.A. he was feeling quite proud of himself. He was now within range of campus and, though definitely feeling tired, he was sure his plan had come off without a hitch. Nearing campus, Sterling knew he would definitely have to take at least a quick power nap once he was back—clearly, he sensed, he was ready to fall asleep at any moment.

Letting his mind drift off to charming visions of his soft pillow and comfortable bed, Sterling hardly realized he was already falling asleep as he waited at a red light just off campus. By the time the light turned green Sterling's consciousness had slipped off into a beguiling dream of his new beer adventures, even as cars behind him honked and maneuvered around his now-stopped vehicle. Fading further into deep sleep, Sterling was shocked when a loud honking noise awakened him suddenly from his reverie. Before he could fully take in what was happening, a figure appeared, tapping insistently on his window. Lowering the window, Sterling caught sight of a charming young woman before him. Straightening himself up in the seat, Sterling tried to turn on the charm but it was clear this particular girl was going to have none of it.

"Excuse me," she exclaimed. "Do you know that you are sitting in front of an intersection. I very nearly ran into you and so did several other cars before me! What are you thinking?!"

"Um, well," Sterling managed to stammer. "I was almost home and felt a little tired."

"I can see," the young woman said, her voice calming as she observed clearly Sterling's exhausted, drooping eyes. "I'm glad I was able to stop before I hit you. I hope you're able to get home ok."

"Thanks so much," Sterling added, genuinely grateful for her kindness.

"I'm Tess, by the way," the young woman added.

"Thanks, Tess," Sterling said warmly, reaching out to shake Tess' hand. "I'm Sterling." Now more fully awake and regaining his usual swagger, Sterling added with a playful wink, "Maybe we'll meet again sometime."

Gunning the car's engine, Sterling powered through the intersection as the light turned green, leaving Tess with a bemused sense of incredulity, certain that the guy she had just encountered was kind of a fool, and yet there was something about him she couldn't help feeling drawn to. In any case, Tess thought, it was highly unlikely they would run into each other again. Not a bad guy, she concluded, but it would take a minor miracle for them to meet again on such a large campus. If it was meant to be, Tess thought, it would happen. She would just have to wait and see.

Chapter 7

Sterling's fraternity's reputation for "Let the good times roll" was in trouble, and he knew that he had to act fast. Gathering together several of his housemates, Sterling called a meeting to set up a plan. The first step would be to find a place to permanently house the supplies for his nascent beer-making operation. To begin with, they would need to clear out the fraternity house basement of years' worth of accumulated junk. From there he would need to set up the bottles and other containers to store the fermenting liquids. It would take weeks for the operation to get off the ground, but Sterling was determined and grateful to have the support of several fellow pledges.

As the younger Sterling set about organizing the operation, Sterling's older self, along with Chris, was having a good laugh taking in the unfolding action.

"Pretty clever, I must say," Chris quipped with amusement.

"Yeah, not bad," Sterling laughed. "I swear I never would have thought of doing it if it hadn't been for the alcohol ban. At that point I was too lazy to do much of anything. It's funny how feeling so motivated to work on that project seemed to get me going again."

"You're right," Chris replied. "This was the beginning of a brilliant career in the liquor business."

"You got that right," Sterling said with pride.

"It's just that you haven't stopped since then, Sterling," Chris added. "Maybe it's time you looked a little closer at what was going on around you."

"I suppose that's true," Sterling responded. "All I know is that it's a kick reliving some of this."

Chris smiled amusedly in response as the scene once more changed around them. Leaving behind the fraternity basement in its embryonic beer-making state, the surroundings slowly morphed into another setting from the frat house very familiar to Sterling: the large backyard. Host to many social events, the yard offered the perfect space for large gatherings. This particular night was one immediately recognizable to the older Sterling. Scanning the room and taking in the scene, he knew right away that this was the night, a few weeks after the initial meeting with his fraternity brothers, of the house's first big event of the year. Dozens of members of the house were there, mingling with countless others from other fraternities and sororities. The music was loud, the beer was flowing, and people were having a great time. It was the perfect culmination for his project, and the young Sterling was feeling exceedingly happy with himself. This surely was what it was all about. This was what college should be.

Wandering amiably around the yard, Sterling chatted with his friends, made sure their bottles were full, and generally basked in the glow of the admiration he had won for himself. Eventually, noticing that the supply of beer bottles was dwindling, Sterling made his way toward the basement and down the stairs to bring up a fresh supply. Opening the door and starting on his way down, he was startled to hear the familiar clinking of bottles being gathered at the bottom of the stairs. "Impossible," Sterling practically shouted as he bolted the rest of the way down the steps. This was not going to be good. Someone had clearly found a way to break the lock on the back room door and discovered his stash. All he could think of was to hope it was just a member of another frat that could be put in his place. At worst, it could be the campus police, but he'd worry about that when he got to the end of the staircase. His precious brew was at stake and there was no time to lose.

"Nah, nothing's impossible." These were the much unexpected words Sterling took in as he rounded the corner at the bottom of the stairs and rushed headlong into a most unexpected sight. Rather than a wayward pledge or a menacing campus narc, the source of the reply was a striking young woman, standing before Sterling holding a case of beer bottles with a look of mixed bemusement and annoyance. In fact, as Sterling processed the sight, he remembered clearly who she was.

"Tess!" he exclaimed. "No way! How is this possible? And what are you doing?!" Sterling managed to get out, as he came to a dead stop at Tess' feet.

"Sterling!" Tess, stammered. "This is definitely a surprise! I see that you're a lot more awake now," Tess said teasingly. "It's great to see you again, but I hate to say that the beer was running low and whoever's hosting this party is clearly not on the ball. I brought my Delta Gamma sisters here and I expect them to have a good time. Wasn't about to let a lot of frat boys get in their way."

"But what do you think you're doing?!" Sterling replied with exasperation. "This is *my* supply. *I* made it. You can't just come in here and take it!"

"Meh," the girl said with a shrug and a smile. "You didn't do a bad job. It's pretty good stuff. Not my fault, though, if you're too busy doing keg stands to take care of your own party."

"But . . . but . . ." Sterling was at a loss for words as the girl let out an amused laugh and brushed past him, carrying his bottles toward the stairs. Stammering, he finally managed to shout out a question as she was walking up.

"Can we at least get together sometime?" Sterling added, "so we can finally be more properly introduced. I promise I will make some beer. And you won't have to break in to get it!"

"Sure," Tess replied, turning her head with a smile. "I'm a physical therapy major. Think I've also seen you in one of my science classes, but then again not very often! Maybe I'll see you in class, or maybe at your next party. Oh, and by the way, you might want to think about getting a better lock next time. Was a cinch to pick."

With that Tess made her way up the stairs, leaving Sterling with a wide-mouthed expression of astonishment on his face, and a feeling somewhere between hatred and wonder that he knew he'd never experienced before. Whoever she was, Sterling was sure that he had to see Tess again, if only to figure out how she'd managed to steal her way into what he'd thought was a secure and sealed-off basement.

As the older Sterling observed the scene, he slowly noticed his surroundings begin to shift around him. From the musty confines of the frat house basement, the scene gradually changed back to his parent's home and vineyard back in northern California. Wondering where the next step of the adventure would take him, Sterling looked to Chris, who stood beside him, smiling. Anticipating Sterling's next question, Chris interjected with a response.

"You might not remember it, Sterling, but there's a very important part of the story that took you from where you were in that basement that night to where you ended up just a few years later," Chris said.

"Hmm, I guess there was a lot that happened, but I was already starting to think ahead to my contract—you know, to produce the beer," Sterling replied.

"Yes, that's true, Sterling," Chris responded, "but do you remember how you go to that point? Do you remember where you got the idea?"

Puzzled momentarily, Sterling thought for a moment and then it came to him. Of course—it was obvious why they were back at the vineyard now. Sterling felt a rush of nostalgia as the idea came to him. It was his younger sister, of course, who had given him the idea. Mindy was special in so many ways. The older Sterling still saw her once in a while but, once again, he had to admit he hadn't invested much time recently in their relationship.

Mindy was now a highly functioning young woman who still lived at the vineyard, helping out with the daily operation and leading tours for enthusiastic tourists and wine experts. It had been Mindy, of course, Sterling remembered, who he had first told about his underground bootlegging business. He was home for Christmas break the semester after his spectacular debut as a beer maker and he couldn't wait to share the news. He was pretty sure his parents would be displeased, to say the least, and so he shared it with the one person he could always count on: his sister. Mindy was always perceptive and patient—a trustworthy confidant—and when they were growing up, both Mindy and Sterling always felt like they could share what was going on in their lives with each other.

This trip home for Sterling was no different. On one of his first nights home that Christmas, Sterling took Mindy aside and told her the good news. Laughing out loud uncontrollably, Mindy had to run into another room when Sterling shared the story.

"So that's what we sent you to college for, Sterling?" Mindy managed to get out as she tried to contain her laughter. "Well, why don't you make the most of it?"

"What do you mean, Mindy?" Sterling replied. "It's just a hobby, and a great way to attract the ladies."

"That's right, Sterling," Mindy responded with a smile. "But you can go big with this. You can sell your recipe!"

"Hmm, I guess so," Sterling replied, thinking through it.

"Definitely," Mindy asserted. "You know the people Mom and Dad sell their wine to. Talk with them and see what they say."

"Not a bad idea, Mindy—thanks!"

Mindy winked and nodded her approval, still losing the battle to contain her amusement over the thought of her brother running an underground beer operation.

Not a bad idea, indeed. The older Sterling knew it, and knew just how right Mindy had been. It wasn't good, he thought, that he'd let so much distance grow between him and his sister. He still helped to pay for her salary and living expenses at the vineyard, but the more this journey was progressing, the more he was starting to realize that money just wasn't enough.

As it turned out, though, money had been very much on Sterling's mind at the beginning of his new venture. In reflection, the older Sterling remembered how excited he had begun to feel at the prospect of what Mindy was suggesting—a genuine family business that would expand the market; not only for his new beer, but even for the wine from the vineyard, and any number of other possibilities. The sky was really the limit, and the younger Sterling was ready to take his business to the next level.

The problem was, of course, money—funds, that is, to get the business off the ground and make his dream a reality. It was with this dilemma in mind that the older Sterling relaxed and smiled as he remembered what had happened next. Glancing knowingly at Chris, neither of them needed to say a word; they both knew the next scene.

"I can't believe I didn't think of it myself," Sterling mused with a smile.

"You can't have all the good ideas, Sterling!" Chris laughed as the scene changed around them.

Once again they were back at the farm, one year later. A few months after his conversation with Mindy, Sterling had mentioned the idea to his parents, who offered their support. They were willing to contribute what they could, but their business at that point was a small one. They had earned the trust of a small, faithful clientele, but they were far from a powerhouse winery along the lines of many others in the more well-known Sonoma and Napa regions. They could help Sterling a bit, but the onus of the work and the financing would be on him.

It was with that in mind that Sterling had returned home again, hoping for something that might give him a lead. As it turned out, he didn't have far to look. On his first night back, at his parents' annual Christmas party for the staff and workers at the winery, Sterling ran into a welcome and familiar face. As they all had grown older, Sterling had seen less and less of Ignacio and Leti, his friends from childhood growing up on the farm; in fact, as Sterling saw them, he couldn't recall what it was that they were each doing, now that all three friends were in college or beyond. He didn't have to wait long to find out.

"Sterling!" shouted Leti as she ran smiling toward her old friend, giving him a big hug. "It's been forever. How are you doing? What have you been up to?"

"I'm great, Leti," Sterling replied, happy to see his friends again and a bit sad that it had been so long.

"Sterling! Bro, how are you?" Ignacio also called out as he came over to embrace his friend.

"Ignacio, it's been way too long," Sterling replied. "How are you guys doing? What are you all doing now?"

"Sterling, it's crazy," Ignacio responded with a smile. "I'm just about ready to graduate. As of May I'll have my degree in business, and I'm ready to take on the world!"

"And don't you remember, Sterling?" Leti chimed in. "I graduated last year and am starting law school. I want to help people like Mom and Dad who didn't have anything when they got to this country. I want to make a difference for them."

"Wow, you guys are both doing so great!" Sterling replied. "I'm jealous! I'm just a lowly sophomore at school and already managed to get kicked off the team and lose my scholarship. I'm hanging on, but I don't know where it's all leading, to tell you the truth."

"Sorry to hear that, man," Ignacio responded.

"Yeah, that's pretty rough," Leti added sympathetically. "You're a resourceful guy, though. I know you'll get through this and land on your feet. What other things do you have lined up?"

"Well, nothing yet really," Sterling replied. "You guys will laugh, but the one thing I didn't completely mess up at school was the fraternity that I joined and the home brew beer I started making for them. It's a hit on campus!"

"No way!" both Ignacio and Leti responded with a collective laugh. "That is too funny!" Leti said, trying to contain herself.

"Yeah, I know," Sterling replied. "But you know what? The hilarious thing is that Mindy thinks I might actually have something there. She thinks I should start marketing the beer and make a business out of it. It's crazy but hey, at this point I'm thinking that may be my best option!"

Both Ignacio and Leti stopped mid-laugh and looked at each other, each seemingly able to read the other's mind.

"Sterling, that's not a bad idea at all," Ignacio said, as Leti nodded her head in agreement, "Heck, you've got us too—a budding entrepreneur and a lawyer-in-the-making. Maybe we can all go in on it together."

"Wow, I don't know what to say," Sterling replied. "That would be incredible. Are you both really up for that?"

"Are you kidding?" Leti spoke with a smile. "You're like our brother. You know we've got your back. Plus, it's a heck of an idea. Certainly can't hurt to try, at least."

"Well, then I guess it's settled," Sterling responded. "Time to start brewing some beer!"

All three friends raised their glasses and toasted to the prospect of the new adventure before them. As they did, the older Sterling and Chris looked on, smiling just as brightly. For all the painful memories he'd encountered so far, Sterling felt like giving thanks for a moment where the happiness he was seeing and remembering finally matched, even if just for a little while, what he felt in that moment, too.

Chapter 8

THE OLDER STERLING WASN'T at all surprised when the next scene from his past appeared before him. Having just relived those all-important moments when the beer-making venture had come together, it only made sense to visit the next significant moment—one that would prove crucial with hindsight, but which came as quite a shock at the time.

It was a few months after Sterling's meeting with Leti and Ignacio, and he was back on campus, into the familiar routine once more of a lackluster attitude toward his classes and a gleeful excitement at his true passion—developing and perfecting a formula for the beer that he was sure would not only help his fraternity throw amazing parties, but also might just help him to make it big—after all, he was quite proud of himself for the 50 percent above-cost rate he was starting to charge for kegs of his home brew. What Sterling wasn't counting on was just how big a splash he would indeed make, and how soon it was destined to occur.

It was late in the semester, and Sterling had been having quite a lot of success so far with the beer. There had been a number of parties he'd supplied for right there in the house, and he was even starting to branch out, providing kegs for other houses and developing something of a reputation on campus. He was riding high, and was looking forward to filling in his friends that summer on how well their project was going.

And then it happened—though even as he looked back on it with some distance, the older Sterling still felt a bit foggy on how exactly it all played out. It was late on a Friday night—or, rather, very early on a Saturday morning—and Sterling had just crashed in his room on the second floor of the frat house, exhausted yet exhilarated from another successful night of intoxication and successful business expansion. He was just about to close his eyes in exhaustion when suddenly he heard his name shouted out with the kind of force and urgency that could only signal some kind of very serious crisis.

"Sterling!!" It was one of his fraternity brothers and Sterling knew something was seriously wrong. Rushing down the stairs, he scanned the hallway below, not bothering to look at what awaited him at the bottom of the last step. Careening down at breakneck speed, Sterling was totally unprepared for the shock he received as his bare feet hit the floor and, rather than touching down on the usual worn shag carpet, slid right into a pool of water several inches deep. His feet both slipping precariously, Sterling quickly found himself flat on his back, sliding across the floor before the large wooden front door unceremoniously arrested his progress with a loud thud.

"Nice work, Sterling!" Chris chortled.

Startled almost as much as his younger self, still laid out on the floor, the older Sterling looked next to him to see Chris doubled over with laughter.

"You really didn't see that coming, did you?" Chris managed to get out. "It's like you stepped on a banana peel and then kept flying!"

"Ha ha, very funny," the older Sterling replied to his friend as he surveyed his younger self struggling to pick himself up off the floor. "It sure didn't feel that hilarious at the time."

And for the younger Sterling, it certainly was a shock. Wrestling himself back to his feet, Sterling stood and surveyed the house. It was incredible—the entire first floor, everywhere he could see, was completely flooded. It was as if a raging tide had crested outside the house and was slowly ascending upward. Dumbfounded, Sterling sloshed over the soggy carpeting toward the kitchen and dining room area, where he could hear the voices of his fraternity brothers expressing similar disbelief.

"Sterling, what the hell happened?!" said one friend as he entered the room.

"I have no idea, man. Why are you asking me?" Sterling replied, still too shocked to take in what was happening.

"Because it's your beer machine downstairs that did it!"

"What?"

"That's right. Apparently you didn't seal the pipe too well there in the kitchen when you spliced it to send more water downstairs. The seal broke and it's been pumping water onto the floor all night!!"

"I can't believe it," Sterling replied in disbelief. "That's impossible."

"Oh, it's possible, man!" another brother shouted at Sterling. "It's not only possible, it happened, and it's your fault!"

"Yeah Sterling, we're screwed, you know," still another friend added. "There's no way we can cover this up. The administration is going to hear about it, and we're going to lose our registration as a house. This is it, man—thanks a lot."

And it was true. The older Sterling knew it of course much more acutely than the younger Sterling was able to grasp in the moment. He remembered well what happened after that fateful night. His fraternity brothers had been correct. And yet the older Sterling felt a stirring of pride as he watched the scene continue to unfold, remembering as he looked on how his younger self had responded.

"Well, you know what, man," the younger Sterling spoke, pulling himself together and addressing his fraternity brother with quiet recognition, "you're right. I really did mess up, and I take responsibility for it." These were words the young Sterling was not at all accustomed to saying. And yet somehow they rolled off his tongue in a way that felt real. Looking around, feeling the water lap around his feet as he moved across the inundated floor, Sterling sensed what he could only describe as liberation. He had been running, swimming, partying, and generally careening through life for so long that there was something radical about simply standing there in the midst of the flood and realizing that something had to give. Sterling had no idea what the change would look like exactly. Would he be kicked out of school? Would he find another place to go? What would the future bring? Sterling had no idea, but somehow he knew, standing transfixed in the flooded house, that *this* was the way forward, right there slogging through the water, finding his way to the drain and then the broom closet for a mop. It would be a long road ahead, wherever it would lead, but Sterling knew this was the way to go.

As it turned out, that very day the administration found out about the incident, revoked the fraternity's approval for the school year, and ruled the group collectively responsible for the substantial cleanup and repair bills that awaited them. What was more, Sterling was called before the university disciplinary board and, in light of the loss of his swimming scholarship, his negligence at the house, plus his illegal brewing business, promptly expelled.

It was a low point, and yet the older Sterling knew where Chris was taking him, even with this painful memory. He knew that precisely at this most acute nadir, when all seemed to be lost, a flicker of hope would appear and carry him forward. As it turned out, this promise of a way out came in the form of three people—Leti, Ignacio, and Tess—three friends who would turn out to play crucial roles in the subsequent unfolding of events.

The next scene was one the older Sterling could have predicted. Opening his eyes, Sterling found himself back at home at his parent's house. It had been several months now since his expulsion from school, and the older Sterling remembered the hard times that had accompanied those first few weeks—sensing he had let his parents down, missing his friends, feeling trapped with little to do except work around the farm.

Thankfully, however, Sterling was not alone. Ignacio and Leti were both still living in the area, studying and pursuing their goals.

It was they who had spent time with Sterling when he got back, trying to be supportive, and who were the important protagonists of the next scene the older Sterling was about to witness.

All three of them were out one night at the local coffee house in town, Ignacio and Leti each working on schoolwork, and Sterling just trying to entertain himself and avoid the tedium of life on the farm. Taking a break from the legal theory book she was reading, Leti looked over at Sterling with a mixture of concern and amusement.

"Sterling," Leti called out, "What are you going to do with yourself? Do you have any kind of plan? You can't just live in the coffee house, you know?"

"Meh," Sterling replied with a shrug. "I really don't know what else I can do. I forfeited my swim scholarship, I ruined my frat house, and I got kicked out of school. What else is there for me to do?"

"You know, Sterling," Ignacio chimed in with equal firmness, "you've gotta figure a way to stop moping around so much. Yes, you've had a hard time of it. Yes, you messed up pretty big time. But, man, don't let it get to you so much. You still have a whole lot of potential. There are so many things you can do."

"Yeah right," Sterling grumbled. "Like what?"

"If you think about it," Leti added, "in the midst of that whole sorry story of your very brief college education, what was the one thing that you really enjoyed, that really gave you energy?"

"Oh, I don't know," Sterling mumbled.

"Of course you do," Leti responded. "It couldn't be more obvious! The one thing you really excelled at, water pipes aside, was the beer brewing you were doing. You loved it, and I know you were really good at it."

"Eh, I guess," Sterling replied.

"I don't guess, I *know* it's true, Sterling," Ignacio added. "Leti's right. You shouldn't give up on that. Remember? We were already starting to talk about going in on it together. Just because you had a technical difficulty doesn't mean we all can't try again. We should give it a shot. We could do amazing things with it."

"I don't know, I suppose so," Sterling responded noncommittally.

"No, it's true," Leti affirmed. "Like we've been saying all along, we can help you. If you get started on making your beer again we can help you. We can make a go of it together."

This idea was the first good news Sterling had heard in a long time. It sparked something in him that had been dormant ever since the series of disasters that had led to his expulsion. This was something new. This was something that really did have potential. Looking back on it, the older Sterling realized that this was a true turning point in his life—a moment that would change things for good.

Chapter 9

THE WARM CALIFORNIA SUN was high in the sky, and a slight breeze caressed the long rows of vines in his family's vineyard as the older Sterling alighted on the next scene. He remembered it well. Looking around, he caught sight of his younger self there in the old barn at the back of the property. Not long after Leti and Ignacio's moment of intervention and encouragement, Sterling had in fact decided to give the beer brewing business another try. His parents weren't thrilled with the idea, but they'd decided at least to give him a chance for the next few months, until the summer ended and he either found a steady job or transferred to a community college.

Consigned to the empty barn at the back of the vineyard, Sterling had steadily begun recreating his successful setup from the frat house. He had the basics of the apparatus arranged and, having learned from his previous mistake, he was working on routing the plumbing in a way that would avoid future catastrophes. With Leti and Ignacio's ongoing encouragement, Sterling was more and more convinced that the business was going to take off. All the right ingredients and components were there—a great product and all kinds of potential for future markets abounded. The only thing missing was the financing. Somehow Sterling was going to have to figure out a way to get the funds he needed, not just to complete the setup in the barn, but ultimately to market, transport, and sell his product in the long-term. He had the dream, and the growing confidence and enthusiasm he knew he would need to make it come true. It was just the practical aspect that still looked pretty uncertain. It was into this situation of both incipient confidence and nagging doubt that a visitor arrived that afternoon at the farm—an unexpected yet welcome guest who would supply the key to finally turning Sterling's vision from a dream into reality.

Kicking up clouds of dust as it made its way speedily over the dirt road that led from the main house to the barn, Sterling noticed a car approaching in the distance. At first he didn't recognize it in the glare of the afternoon sun and the dusty haze that framed its gradual progress towards him. As it drew nearer, though, Sterling felt his jaw drop in complete but pleasant surprise. At first it seemed too unreal to believe, but it was true. Unmistakably, it was his friend Tess' dark blue convertible, and its driver appeared clearly in view as well—none other than Tess herself.

Sterling couldn't believe it. In his shamed rush to leave campus after the debacle of the accident at his frat house, he hadn't said goodbye to almost any of his friends. A few of them he emailed or called later, but with many, Tess most especially, Sterling felt entirely too humiliated. Why bother, in any case, he wondered. No doubt, once Tess discovered how much of a loser he was, she would have lost interest in him as a friend, much less anything else. Since they had met that night at the frat house, they had been hanging out more and more. Though Sterling was perennially occupied with his beer-making and partying, there was something special about the times they had spent together. And yet, now it was probably all for naught. It was best just to make a clean break and not subject himself to the embarrassment of her rejection.

It was with visible shock, then, that Sterling stared at the car as it approached, and at its smiling occupant. Pulling over toward the side of the barn, Tess turned off the engine, rotated her head slowly toward Sterling, and without missing a beat, let out an uproarious laugh. Still too overwhelmed to speak, Sterling stared on as Tess opened the car door, stood up, and walked toward him. Noticing his visible surprise, Tess let out another friendly chuckle and finally spoke.

"Now Sterling," she said with a smile. "You really didn't think you could get rid of me that easily, did you?"

"Ah ... um ..." Sterling simply didn't know what to say.

"I heard about the epic flood at the house and came over later that day to try and find you. Your roommate said you'd already gone, and when I emailed you and tried to call, I never heard back."

"I'm really sorry, Tess," Sterling replied, finally finding a few words to say amidst his surprise to see her.

"It's okay, Sterling," Tess responded. "I was hurt at first, but I knew that couldn't have been an easy thing for you to go through. You were probably embarrassed and wanted to get as far away from there as possible. I wanted to find you though, just so you know that I still think you're a cool guy and that you're not alone in this. Heck, I might even be able to help you, if you still want to work on your beer. Many years back, before he passed away, my grandfather gave me a little bit of money that he said I should invest. I've been saving it and investing it here and there over the years. It's not a lot, but it would be a start."

If Sterling had been surprised before, he was positively speechless now. If he had planned exhaustively in advance, he could not have come up with a more perfect scenario for procuring precisely what he needed in exactly the right moment. Sterling wasn't sure if he believed in miracles, but this was surely about as close as you could get.

Looking off into the distance with wonder and taking in the scene, the older Sterling (with Chris standing, a knowing smile on his face, right next to him) was starting to lose whatever doubts his younger self had had—miracles did indeed happen, and more and more, he was seeing that they were all around him.

Chapter 10

A FEW MONTHS HAD passed by the time of the next scene that Chris and the older Sterling visited. With Tess' moral and financial support, Sterling had successfully replicated the beer-making setup he had constructed at the frat house, though this time in the much safer and less flood-prone barn at the back of his parents' property.

Already producing several different varieties of beer, Sterling had even managed to recruit his parents to the project. Though more than a bit skeptical at first, his mom and dad had come around in what Sterling knew was the best way possible—they actually tasted the beer and really liked it.

"Not bad at all, Sterling," his father had remarked with a combination of amusement and admiration.

"Actually, it's really good," his mom added. "This is high-quality stuff."

"Well, his name is Sterling, right?" Sterling's sister Mindy exclaimed. "That's what his name means, something that's really good!"

"Aw, sis, you're so sweet," the younger Sterling called out to Mindy, reaching over to give her a hug. "I'm thrilled that you guys all like it so much," he continued. "I was really starting to get depressed, and I know I disappointed you all with everything that happened back at school. I know it might not look like the most worthwhile thing to be doing, especially in light of all that happened, but it's funny—I feel like making beer is actually what I was meant to be doing all along. It kind of just fits."

"That's really great, Sterling," his mom replied. "And you know what? That's all that really matters anyway. That's all any of us want for you—that you find something that you enjoy doing and that's meaningful for you."

"Absolutely, son, if making beer is what feels right and makes sense for now, then go for it," Sterling's dad added. "In fact, your mom and I were just talking earlier today about the wine growers' conference we go to each year that's coming up. Why don't you come with us and bring some samples of your beer. Who knows, you might pique some interest with some of the other owners."

"Yeah, Sterling, you might make an even bigger splash than you did—literally—in college!" Mindy added with a wry smile as Sterling and his parents all laughed contagiously at the humorous truth of Mindy's observation.

Taking in the scene from afar, the older Sterling and Chris shared in the laughter, though for Sterling it was an amusement tinged with a hint of ambivalence. He knew how prescient his family had been in that moment, yet none of them could have predicted just how quickly things would develop. Chris, sensing Sterling's thoughts, interrupted with a question.

"Sterling," Chris interjected. "I believe I have an idea of what you're thinking about."

"Yeah," Sterling replied. "I figured you would."

"A penny for your thoughts," Chris added with a kind smile.

"Well, you know, it's just that—who could have known how fast things were going to go, right?" Sterling replied. "I mean, there I was, having just been kicked out of my first year of college, with no money, no future, and no hope, and thanks to Tess, Mindy, Leti, Ignacio, Mom, and Dad, I had a few dozen bottles of beer and the barest hope that something might come of it. Who could have predicted that I'd meet Mr. Rafael at that conference. I mean, what were the odds?"

"You're absolutely right, Sterling," Chris responded. "It was pretty amazing. There you were, a punk kid fresh out of the frat house, and you run into one of the most important winemakers in

Napa Valley. He sees—or rather tastes—something special in the beer that you brought to the conference and offers you a job right then and there. Granted, it was in middle management, but it was at his flagship vineyard in Napa, and he knew he had something special in you."

"Yeah, I guess it was only a few years before I was the general manager of the whole operation," Sterling added. "I mean, it's crazy, right? I go from making beer in a basement to working with some of the greatest winemakers in the world in just a matter of a few years!"

"You're right, Sterling. It was crazy. It was lucky. It was amazing. It was also an opportunity that very few people ever get in this life," Chris interjected.

"Yeah, I know," Sterling replied. "I guess I did seize the opportunity, right? Look, here I am—well, I guess, wherever we are. In any case, I'm a huge success. I've made it, right? I've got an amazing job, I travel all over the world, I provide a product that makes a lot of people happy, and on top of it I make enough money to send lots back to the family. I even managed to rename the company after myself. That's not so bad, is it?"

"You tell me, Sterling," Chris responded. "You're right that you've made it many ways. You've got all you could possibly want."

"But is it enough?" Sterling interjected. "I feel like there's still something I'm missing. I mean, I don't think I was aware of it until now, but this crazy journey through time with you—well, it's definitely putting some things in perspective. I don't know what it all means yet, but I know there's a lesson in all of this somewhere."

"Perceptive as always," Chris replied with a grin. "The lesson is all around you. Maybe just one more stop on our little tour will do the trick."

"You know I'm game, Chris," Sterling replied. "If you've taken me this far, you've gotta have an idea of where this is all going."

"Maybe, just maybe." Chris laughed as the scene began to shift around them once more."

Chapter 11

As the scene changed, Sterling had a feeling that they were nearing the end of their journey. He could almost sense that things were coming full circle, and yet that there was perhaps still one last lesson to be learned. Ruminating on what the lesson could be, Sterling started to recognize where they were.

"This is my parents' house, in their kitchen," Sterling observed as the scene came into view.

"You bet," Chris chimed in with a smile. "How observant!"

"Very funny," Sterling laughed. "But where is everybody?"

"Just watch, Sterling," Chris commented. "You'll see."

As Chris finished speaking, the front door opened and Sterling's sister Mindy walked through, carrying the day's mail. From upstairs, Sterling heard his mother call out to Mindy.

"Anything new today, Mindy?"

"No just the usual. Some bills, some credit card offers. Oh, and big surprise—another check from Sterling."

Mindy walked in to the kitchen with the mail in hand, and leaving everything else on the table, made her way over to a cabinet drawer and opened it. Inside, Sterling could make out a large stack of unopened letters, all of them clearly the checks he had been sending his family over the past several years.

Astonished and not sure what to think, Sterling turned around and saw his mother come down the stairs and into the kitchen.

"Yeah, can't say I'm too surprised either," his mother responded. "I know Sterling means well, but he just doesn't get some things. For us it's never been about the money. We do okay with our business and that's what your father and I want. Sterling has made a name for himself and that's great—but that's his business. It just would be nice to actually *see* him once in a while."

"Yup," Mindy nodded in agreement. "It's like he thinks he can pay us so he doesn't have to feel guilty for never showing up anymore."

"I hate to say it, but you're right, Mindy," Sterling's mother added. "I really miss him and I know your father does, too. It's amazing how just seeing someone and spending time together makes such a huge difference. It truly is something that money could never buy."

Sterling observed the scene and felt a tear starting to well up in his eye. Not wanting to look over at Chris, he kept his gaze fixed on the scene before them. Chris, however, could see what was happening.

"It's okay, Sterling," Chris whispered with tenderness, placing his strong hand on Sterling's shoulder." "It's a good thing to cry. It shows that you're human. It means that you're getting in touch with things you haven't had time to feel in a long, long time. Tears can be very cathartic."

"Yeah," Sterling managed to get out, wiping away the tears now cascading down his cheeks. "It's been too long."

"It probably has, Sterling," Chris added. "But it's never too late. There's still plenty of time, if you take advantage of it.

"I want to, Chris," Sterling said with conviction. "I need to. I just need to see one more thing. Please take me to see Tess. I know I haven't been the best support to her either."

"Yes, that's true, Sterling," Chris agreed. "Close your eyes and when you open them we'll be there with her."

Closing and then opening his eyes once more, Sterling began to recognize another familiar scene. It was his office. The headquarters of Sterling Enterprises, Inc., now an internationally known and respected brand. As the scene came into view, Sterling recognized the familiar features of one of the conference rooms, just down the hall from his office. As he and Chris took their places at the back, Tess, who helped from time to time with consulting, and one of the sales associates, Amy, came in, midway through what seemed to be an emotional exchange.

"You know, Amy," Tess confessed with evident pain. "I really think I've had enough. I mean, how long has it been? Almost ten years? I met him in college. I helped him get this business off the ground after he was *expelled* from school. I moved in with him and have been loyal and faithful to him. I've pursued my physical therapy career and still put in quite a lot of time here supporting him and his company. Yes, we got engaged, and I've stood by him all this time, but where is this all going?"

"Has he even talked about when you're getting married?" Amy asked.

"Yeah, he's mentioned it. We've talked about it a few times, but it's always the same excuse. He's too busy, he has too many commitments. He has to go to an international conference. He has to spend time expanding the company. I mean I understand that he has aspirations and goals—and really that's a great thing. But it's like sometimes he can't see that there are other things in life besides work and making more money. I've got this five-carat rock on my finger and no hope of a wedding day."

"Right," added Amy. "Like an amazing, beautiful, and wonderful woman sitting right in front of his nose who he doesn't appreciate in the slightest."

"Yeah, I sure feel that way sometimes," Tess said in agreement.

"Well, yeah! It's been the better part of a decade and he doesn't have the decency to make a commitment to you. If it were me, I'd be shaking the dust off my feet and heading to somewhere and someone a lot more appreciative."

Cracking a smile, Tess nodded in agreement.

Once more Sterling took in the scene, sensing a wave of emotion well up from deep within. Again the tears started to flow, but this time there was something different. Sterling could feel that a part of him deep inside had changed. In a strange yet powerful way, he sensed that he wasn't the same person he had been at the start of this extraordinary journey he had embarked on with Chris.

"I know it, too, Sterling," Chris said with a smile.

"Know what?" Sterling asked, incredulous.

"Know that you're not the same—that you've been transformed."

"How do you do that?!" Sterling asked with astonishment.

"Ah, just a little something I've picked up along the way. I know you're soon going to see as well, Sterling, that when you help people—when you really open your heart to them, you find treasures you can't begin to imagine."

"You know, I'm starting to imagine them, Chris. Just starting—but I think I'm beginning to get the idea."

"I know, Sterling. And I'm incredibly proud of you. You're a quick study!"

"And you're an excellent teacher!"

Seeing Chris look at him with a sort of love and compassion he could feel deeply, Sterling began to cry, and soon felt Chris' strong arms embrace him, almost as if he were both falling and being held at the same time. Soon the scene changed around them and Sterling could start to hear other voices speaking along with Chris'.

"You got him, Chris?"

"Yeah, I just need to unbuckle him. He's basically hanging here in midair. It's a good thing he had his seatbelt on."

Slowly the scene started to come into view for Sterling. He was upside down, looking out the front window of his car and hearing the drone of ambulance sirens in the distance. Looking down, Sterling felt himself being held gently yet firmly, and shook with astonishment when he saw who was holding him tight.

"Chris!" Sterling exclaimed. "It's you!"

"Why, uh, yes," Chris said with a smile. "I'm a paramedic and I'm here to help you get out. I'm going to unbuckle you now. All you need to do is fall down into my arms and let me carry you out."

Nodding his consent, Sterling felt Chris unbuckle his belt and sensed his body falling and yet held in a tight embrace. Before he knew it, Sterling was outside the car and loaded onto the ambulance. As the other paramedics tended to his wounds and prepared to depart, Sterling looked at the doors as they were about to close and noticed that Chris was preparing to shut them.

"Chris," Sterling cried out. "You're not coming?

"No, Sterling," Chris smiled. "You'll be just fine. I got you down; now, the rest of the journey is yours to take."

Smiling, Sterling nodded in agreement. Laying his head down on the ambulance stretcher, Sterling knew that, indeed, the journey was just beginning. There was still so much to process—so much to do and so much to say to so many. And yet, somehow Sterling knew that Chris had been right. It really was all about the people— people he may have neglected or taken for granted before, but people who had stood by him nevertheless. He knew it might take awhile to mend some of those relationships, to put back together some of the broken pieces, but deep down he also knew, like Chris had said, that the journey would take him where he needed to go. Really, in the end, it was just a matter of sitting back, taking it all a little less seriously, and allowing the road before him to unfold at its own time and pace. Closing his eyes as he had so many times in his travels with Chris, Sterling relaxed onto the bed and waited, knowing that, just as with Chris, the next phase of the journey, while unknown, would without a doubt teach him many things. As he had learned, it was simply a matter of letting go and letting the path arise to teach him, to transform him, to free him.

Chapter 12

FLICKERING, DANCING, SHIMMERING. THERE was light coming from somewhere, and yet Sterling wasn't sure where. After the healing catharsis he had just experienced, he found it odd and disorienting to suddenly be somewhere very different. What had happened? Where was he? And how did he get there?

As Sterling's eyes slowly adjusted to what he was seeing, he gradually could make out a scene of people talking, though there was no sound to be heard. Still confused, with his ears ringing and his head throbbing with what felt like a crushing migraine headache, he strained all the more to try and make out what was happening. Little by little, as the figures danced before his eyes he started to realize he was looking at a TV screen. All else was dark around him, but he could distinguish the outline of the monitor hanging in front of him on the wall. But where was he? What was this place?

Straining to make out any other sights or sounds, Sterling glanced around and listened to the faint hum and occasional beep of machines that seemed to surround him completely. Still perplexed and alternately dizzy and nauseated, Sterling brought his gaze back to the flickering images on the screen, slowly beginning to discern the outlines of his own body beneath a blanket. Finally connecting what he was perceiving with what he was feeling, Sterling realized suddenly what was going on. He was in a bed in a hospital, though he knew not where or why.

Relieved at least to have a vague sense of what was going on, Sterling returned his attention to his form beneath the blanket. Sensing an excruciating rush of pain seemingly in every part of his body, he strained to raise himself up from the bed, but quickly fell back down, seemingly exhausted and aching everywhere. At least able to move his head a bit, Sterling turned his gaze back and forth from left to right several times, taking in all the details he could make out in the room—the flickering television screen, the lights and intermittent noises of the medical equipment surrounding him, the darkness punctuated by dim street lights he could make out through the window, and the outline of a door with a faint light stealing in through the frame and underneath.

It was clear now to Sterling that he was in a hospital room and that it was late at night. No voices or other signs of human presence stirred anywhere and, with searing pain coursing through both every place and no place in particular throughout his body, Sterling felt acutely, unmistakably alone. Steeling himself to try and raise his body one more time, Sterling strained every muscle and lunged upward, only to quickly fall back. Crying out in frustration, he realized that he could hardly make a sound because of the tight dryness in his throat. He could breathe, and yet he perceived a distinct hoarseness and aching as he tried to shout out. Like the rest of his body, his vocal chords were nearly immobile, hardly able to emit the slightest sound that might rouse someone's attention.

Clearly, Sterling was alone, and he had no clue what to do. Glancing around, he made one last attempt to rouse himself from the bed before collapsing in sheer exhaustion. His efforts to sit up were not working, and so he was going to have to think of something else. Exhausted from the exertion, though, the only thing Sterling could summon up was the strange parade of images and emotions he seemed to have just awakened from. Were those things real? Did they actually happen? What was reality and what was a dream? All Sterling knew was that what he had just experienced *felt* utterly real. From the conversations with Chris to the visits to his family's farm and the return to what he had experienced in college, all of it was incredibly real, and yet it strained the limits of credulity. In any case, Sterling surmised, whether what he had experienced was real or not, it was something he needed to give some thought to.

Reviewing all the things he had just seen and felt and learned in his mind, Sterling tried to bring together what seemed most coherent (or at least identifiable) about what he had experienced. In a way, it all started with his time at college. That was where he had met both his greatest opportunities and his most bitter defeats. Starting out with the swimming scholarship, Sterling remembered the exhilaration of his triumphs in the pool, leading the team to a number of victories, even as his career drew to a rapid close with the decisions he now knew he couldn't take back.

And yet there was also a tinge of gratitude that Sterling sensed very deeply laying there in the hospital bed. If it hadn't been for the mistakes he'd made those years before, he knew he never would have found his way to the other series of adventures that had brought him to where he was that day. Without those earlier moments, he never would have met Tess, or had the opportunities that had brought him back into his family's business in the vine-yards of California where he had grown up.

It was all clearly right there before him, Sterling thought. All he ever could have dreamed and hoped for was right there. Granted, he hadn't exactly been seeing it or valuing it much lately, but it was there. His path lay open before him, and he had already embarked upon it. All he needed to do was look around and see it. Now, if only he could get up out of the bed to start walking it.

He started to glance around the room again to see if there was something that he could use to get someone's attention. He noticed that the call button had fallen over the side of the bed, making it impossible to free the cord trapped between the rail and the mat-tress. Then he noticed a bedpan on top of the bedside table. With all of his might he feverishly reached over to grab hold of it, and yet his arms would not do what he wanted them to. It felt as if he were trapped—unable to move, struggling to breathe, stuck in the bed alone. Sensing a wave of despair about to overwhelm him, Sterling wondered when or even if all of this would ever end.

As if on cue, the hospital room door opened gently, as Sterling looked over toward the sliver of light between the dark room and the space of hallway that came into view. There, illuminated and moving toward him, Sterling spotted a figure that seemed mysteriously, yet utterly, familiar. Straining to make out the features of the sudden guest, Sterling slowly distinguished the outlines of a paramedic's uniform. Sterling looked intently as the figure neared him, and the name on his uniform grew visible: Chris. Startled, Sterling immediately returned to the series of moments that had just transpired, all featuring the friendly presence of a friend he had come to know as Chris.

Could there be a connection? Sterling wondered. *Who is this Chris, and who have I spent these moments with, which all seem like a dream now?*

As Sterling wondered, he felt his heart jump inside him as the man now approaching him came into view. Not only was this a medical worker, and not only was his name Chris. This *was* Chris. It was unmistakable; this was the very same person Sterling had been talking to, reflecting with, travelling alongside. This *had* to be the same person.

"Chris!" Sterling exclaimed, surprising himself with his own enthusiasm. "Chris! I can't believe it! How did this happen?"

Startled, the man stopped and raised his eyes toward Sterling with a look of incredulous surprise. "Sterling?! This is incredible! Do you know how long you've been unconscious? It's been five weeks. This is amazing! . . . And . . . ah . . . yes, my name is Chris. Remember, we talked briefly when I pulled you out of the car? I remembered you and checked with your family to see how you were doing. They said you had fallen into a deep sleep and that a visit might be a good thing, so here I am," Chris said with a kind smile.

Even more emboldened, Sterling could hardly contain himself. "Well, of course you're here, and of course I know your name! Think of all the things you and I just went through. How could I not know who you are, and how could I not thank you for all you've done for me?"

"Well, sir . . . ah . . . Sterling . . . I really can't say I've done much," Chris spoke haltingly. "I had the privilege to help you after your accident. You've definitely been through a lot, but I wouldn't say I should get any credit. It's really been you who have fought your way through this. All of us have just been here to support you."

At that moment, throwing open wider the door and flooding the space with light, a group of what seemed to Sterling like a small crowd of people entered into the room. Hearing his name from everywhere, Sterling turned his attention from Chris and started to distinguish the faces of those greeting him. There was his mother and father, his sister Mindy, Ignacio and Leti, and Chris, of course. Incredible as it was, everyone was there. Seemingly everyone he had just dreamed of, or come into contact with, or somehow encountered—all of them were there, speaking his name, embracing him, and sharing with him what he clearly could feel was love. Sterling wasn't sure where he had just been, or how exactly things would continue to unfold from there, but one thing he knew with absolute certainty in that moment: he was loved, and somehow, in the great mystery of what had transpired in those moments, and in the ones that would follow, all would be well.

Chapter 13

AWAKENING TO FIND SUCH a scene of love and support all around him, Sterling felt surprised by the reaction that seemed to well up within him, almost a desire to reach out and embrace his family, including his parents and his sister, and even the hospital staff there surrounding the bed, though he felt his heart ache at the same time for the one person who was not present: Tess. And yet, trying to fulfill the need he felt to reach out, Sterling quickly was reminded that such a move was all but impossible.

Straining to lift himself in the bed and move his arms, Sterling was shocked to confirm his earlier suspicion—that not only could he not raise himself, but that his arms were totally immobile. Straining to lift his head to see what was going on, Sterling gasped as he discerned the outlines of two long white casts stretching from his shoulders all the way to his hands. Both of his arms were fully encased and immobilized in the hospital bed, preventing him from lifting or even rotating them. Searching further down his body, Sterling let out a loud shout of exasperation as he took in the sight of both of his legs likewise bound and encased in full casts.

"Who the *hell* did this?!" he screamed. "*What* are you all trying to do to me?"

Quickly abandoning the serenity he had felt as he started to awaken, Sterling went wild. Falling back into a feeling of helplessness and rage, Sterling lashed out, thrashing around as much as his immobilized body would let him in the hospital bed.

"*Why?*" he shouted as loud as his hoarse voice would permit. "Why did this have to happen to me? Why didn't you all just leave me out there? What good am I going to be to anyone now?"

Flailing back and forth on the bed, Sterling alternately struggled and screamed out in pain as his family, in shock and unsure of what to do, stared at the scene. Finally, Sterling's father took hold of Sterling by the shoulders and tried to shake him out of it.

"Sterling!" his father yelled out. "Sterling, you are going to be alright. You will survive this. It's not the end of the world."

Approaching the bed, Sterling's mother stroked his forehead, now covered in perspiration, and repeated the same words.

"Sterling, you'll be okay," his mother intoned. "It's not going to be easy but you will get through this."

"What do you all care?" Sterling shouted. "Who needs you all anyway? Just leave me alone and I'll take care of it. I've got money. I'll hire somebody to get me the hell out of here and help me until I get better."

"Sterling," his mother interjected. "We know you have plenty of resources; that's not the issue. The reality is that you need help, and who better to take care of you than your own family?"

"Yeah, whatever," Sterling shot back. "Just leave me alone, all of you. I don't need your pity. I don't need your charity. Just get out."

Tears welling up in their eyes, Sterling's parents stepped back from the bed and returned to their seats near the back wall of the hospital room as Sterling continued to moan and attempt to twist himself around in the bed. However, Mindy, opening her eyes wide and letting out an exclamation, suddenly bolted from her seat and ran out the door into the adjoining hallway. Confused and still in shock over what Sterling had said, everyone else remained seated, imagining that Mindy had grown overcome with emotion and just needed to take a break. Before long, however, the family heard Mindy's voice from a distance down the hallway.

As Sterling's family had learned from early on in Mindy's life, she had a gift for music and, in particular, for singing. A member of the local high school choir and a major fan of Broadway musicals,

Mindy had a keen musical ear and loved to share her gift with her family. As the strains of Mindy's singing made their way down the hallway, Sterling recognized immediately the tune she was humming. Taking him back once more to his *abuelo* Alfonso, Sterling remembered immediately where Mindy had first sung the song. Early in their teenage years, when their grandfather passed away, Mindy had insisted that she sing a particular song at his funeral. And not just that she sing it, but that it be a duet, and specifically with her brother. Sterling at the time had thought the idea was crazy, but Mindy persisted until he grudgingly agreed. He hated to admit it at the time, but when Mindy played him the record of the song, Andrew Lloyd Webber's "Pie Jesu," he couldn't help but recognize that it was strikingly beautiful. He had no idea how he would pull it off, but Mindy led the way, and the duet they shared that day lived on in the family's memory as a particularly moving tribute to the memory of their grandfather.

Mindy's voice grew stronger now as she approached the room and Sterling couldn't help but find himself singing along ever so softly in harmony with his sister, feeling his grandfather's spirit somehow present there with him. Finally, as Mindy neared the doorway into the room, she allowed her singing to trail off and then, rounding the corner into the doorway, let out an exclamation: "*Sterling!*" she exclaimed. "Sterling, I have just what you need! I know this will help you!"

Bursting into the room, in her excitement Mindy practically dragged with her a woman with a hospital nametag and a smiling face who also had a special companion in tow.

"Hello, Sterling," the woman said gently. "I hear from your sister Mindy that you may be in need of some extra friendship right now. Accidents are really hard things to face, but no matter what we're going through, it always helps to have friends by our side."

With that the woman pulled her hand forward and with it followed a gigantic, fluffy sheep dog, trotting into the room. Bounding up to the bed, the dog raised its front paws to the side of the mattress and let out a friendly bark. Caught totally by surprise, Sterling's mouth stood agape as the dog nuzzled its nose under his exposed hand at the end of the cast. Stretching out his fingers as best he could, Sterling found himself, almost without knowing it, starting to caress the dog's fur and pet its head nestled snugly next to his hand. And before he could object or say anything further, Sterling suddenly felt tears first trickle, and then gradually stream down his face. Somehow, the love and the care he couldn't bring himself to accept from his family now came rushing to him in the form of an affectionate furry friend. To Sterling, it was patently absurd, and yet it didn't matter. He felt the love flowing in, and he somehow knew he was going to get through whatever it was that lay ahead.

"Sterling, this is Biscuit," the woman spoke warmly as she gently nudged the dog back to her side next to the bed. "She is a companion dog, one of many, in fact, that help us here at the hospital. She is a real friend and such a sweetheart. In fact, she is one of our dogs who is in need of a home base for when she is not working here at the hospital. She is still pretty young, and needs a loving family who can help her to have the care and affection she needs so she can keep doing the amazing things she does here with our patients."

Sterling was still too surprised to say anything, and his parents and other siblings were likewise astonished to see the transformation that Sterling's new friend had made in such a short time. Mindy, however, was less circumspect. Rushing over to the woman and the dog, Mindy embraced both and quickly announced, "We will be her friends! We will take care of her!"

With that Sterling, forgetting the pain in his limbs and the frustration of his immobility, yelled out in support of his sister.

"Yes, Mindy!" Sterling shouted. "You're right! I have no idea why I'm saying this, but I know you're right. We will take Biscuit home!"

Rising from their seats, Sterling's parents quickly crossed toward the bed. His mother arrived first and asked Sterling, "Then you will let us bring you home? You'll come back to the farm to get better?"

"Yes, I will," Sterling responded, his eyes meeting his mother's. "I could do this on my own, but if Mindy wants me to come home, I will."

"Yes!!" Mindy exclaimed. "It's just what I hoped. Sterling is coming home!"

With that, the family gathered around Sterling's bed, taking turns embracing him as Biscuit let out a loud, friendly yelp of approval and Sterling found himself starting to relax into the idea that, maybe, accepting his family's help wouldn't be so bad after all.

Chapter 14

THE CALIFORNIA SUN SHONE brightly, reflecting off cars passing by on the freeway as Sterling gazed out the windows of the medical transport van that was carrying him back toward home. It had been several more weeks, and Sterling was ready for a change from the monotony of the hospital room and the frustration of his immobility. He still had many weeks left in the casts that restrained all his limbs, and yet he longed to break free, to move, to walk, anything that would bring back the the accustomed sense of mobility and autonomy he was starting to fear he may well have lost for good.

Sensing the van turn, Sterling glanced at the scene outside his window and immediately recognized the exit they were taking. It was the road leading from the main highway, US 101, off toward the west and the rolling hills cascading toward the valley where his family's vineyard stood. Sterling knew the road intimately from countless trips as a boy and as a young man working in his family's business, hauling supplies, entertaining clients, and supervising shipments; plus, of course, his all-night mission to secure the beer-making supplies. Yet this time felt different. Now Sterling was returning as an adult, as an independent, successful entrepreneur with countless successes to his name. Still, he was coming back in a position of need, vulnerability, perhaps even helplessness. He despised the feeling, and yet he knew there was little he could do to stem it. Somehow, he would have to figure out a way to get through all of this and forge a path back to the life he had built for himself back south in L.A.

Pulling into the main drive leading through the vineyard toward the family farmhouse in the distance, Sterling admired the precision of the rows of vines, lightly weighted with what would in a few months be a mature harvest to be collected, pressed, and initiated on its way toward eventual transformation into that year's vintage. Sterling had heard this was to be an exceptionally strong year for the grapes and the wine they would produce, and he made a mental note to himself, when he could, to inquire about the progress of the season with some of the workers.

As the van approached the house, Sterling caught himself nearly cracking a smile as he noticed his family descending the main stairs, anxious to meet him on his arrival. For all his reticence about coming back, something in him said this was where he was supposed to be, back home if only for a little while, until he could get back on his feet and back in the game. Opening the van's door, Sterling's father beamed as he shouted out a welcome just as everyone else intoned a similar greeting. Racing ahead of a smiling Mindy and pulling her enthusiastically along, Sterling's unlikely new friend Biscuit bounded up the van's steps, landing her front paws on the side of Sterling's seat and nudging him playfully with her nose. Sterling couldn't help but smile as he greeted Biscuit and the others while the medical transport workers carefully lowered his stretcher and carried him up the main stairs and through the house to the ground floor study that would be his room for the next several weeks.

After his family had all extended their greetings and welcomed him home, Sterling settled into his bed, admiring the sweeping view of the vineyards and the rolling hills before him. As his thoughts drifted between irritation at the prospect of many more weeks of reliance on others and grudging thankfulness for his family's care, a knock came at the bedroom door. Convinced that he had already greeted everyone present on the farm, Sterling rotated his neck and as much of his upper body as he could to try to make out who it was who could be visiting him. Glancing toward the door, he recoiled in disbelief as his eyes met those of the one person he was sure he would not see that day: Tess.

Stepping over the threshold with care yet obstinacy, and before Sterling could utter a word of protest, Tess made her way across the room toward his bed.

"Sterling!" Tess exclaimed as she walked toward him. "You've really done it this time!"

"Tess, what are you doing here?" Sterling shouted in frustration. "You're seriously the last person I ever thought I would see today."

"Well, Sterling," Tess interjected with exasperation, "I guess this is the universe's way of playing a practical joke on both of us."

"Huh?" Sterling responded.

"So it turns out that I'm the physical therapist on duty this week with the agency your health insurance contracted."

"What, you mean, I have no other choice?" Sterling intoned with a note of desperation.

"Funny, that's the same question I asked myself," Tess added. "It turns out that all the other therapists are assigned this week, so if you're interested in getting better and if I want to have a job, then I guess we're both stuck."

"Wow, that is a cosmic joke if there ever was one," Sterling quipped. "Here I am in the worst moment of my life. I barely survive an accident. I wake up in a hospital. I'm stuck at home for who-knows-how-long. And now the person who dumped me for no apparent reason is my self-imposed physical therapist. Wow, what a life!"

"Uh, yeah, Sterling," Tess said with a sigh. "Well, I really don't even know where to begin with all that. You know there were *lots* of reasons why I had to put my foot down and say enough was enough."

"But . . ." Sterling tried to interject.

"I know, Sterling, you're a master at excuses and rationalization, but I'm not even gonna go there today. I'm just going to do my job and then move along. End of story."

"Well," Sterling added. "I guess I'll just have to do the same thing myself. Let's just do this and get it over with."

Nodding in agreement, Tess pulled up a chair to the bed and launched from memory into the presentation she always gave with new patients, introducing them to the fundamentals of physical therapy and the work that they would be doing together as the person healed. As she rattled off the familiar verbiage, however, her mind wandered to the long past the two shared, and she knew that it would not be easy caring as a therapist for someone she had cared for in a deeper fashion for so long, and, who she knew, deep down, she still cared about.

As Tess reflected while she talked, Sterling also listened to her words, but found his thoughts drifting back to happier moments the two had shared together. It wasn't that he no longer cared about Tess. She would always be important to him. It was just that too much had happened between them. Their past seemed just too heavy a burden to overcome. And yet, even as his mind argued against Tess even being there in the first place, something else inside seemed to say there might yet be more to the story.

Over the coming weeks, the physical therapy sessions continued three times a week. Though grudgingly at first, with time Tess felt like she was getting used to the routine. Granted, it wasn't pleasant having to keep going back to her ex's boyhood home, re-encountering his parents, dealing with him, and trying not to think too much about the past. Still, from time to time Tess felt like there was almost something right about what was happening, like maybe it was what they both needed for closure.

One day, several weeks into the program, as Tess was helping Sterling move one of his arms, she surprised herself when a question just seemed to pop out before she could even think much about it.

"Sterling?" she intoned. "What do you think happened?"

"What?" Sterling replied. "What do you mean, what happened?"

"Oh forget about it," Tess responded, trying to hide her embarrassment at the spontaneity of the question. "I don't even know what I meant by that."

"Well, clearly you meant something," Sterling added in response. "What were you referring to?"

"I guess, well," Tess hesitated as the thoughts started coming to her. "Really, what I wanted to know—actually, what I've wanted to ask you for a long time is how it happened that we drifted apart. I mean, I know at the end you were totally distant, literally and figuratively, and that's why ultimately I broke it off. But, I mean, what happened in the first place?"

"Well, I guess it was probably both of us, really," Sterling responded. Normally such a question from Tess or anyone else for that matter would have annoyed him to no end. But even he had to admit that all the quiet time alone and Tess's regular visits had started to soften him. For some reason, the question didn't bother him, and in fact he found himself feeling glad to start the conversation.

"You know," Sterling continued, "when I moved down to L.A., we did the whole long-distance thing for those several years and it kind of worked. But I got busy and I guess we just kind of drifted apart."

"Yeah," Tess added, "you definitely got busy, Sterling. Too busy for me, too busy for your parents and your siblings, too busy for just about anyone from here. And, yeah, you're right that part of it too was kind of a drifting apart. When I saw that you were so busy, then I felt okay focusing more on my career, and I started bothering less and less with coming down to L.A. to see you. I guess before long the relationship just ended before either of us realized it had."

"I think you're right, Tess," Sterling said, nodding in agreement. "Look, I recognize my part in the whole thing, but I think you're right. I mean, I was a pretty lousy boyfriend to you back then, but when I noticed you weren't coming around much anymore, I did miss you. It just felt almost too late at that point, and besides, I was so busy with the company and how successful we were at the time. Really, like you say, we just kind of drifted apart."

"Yeah, that seems right," Tess confirmed. "I mean, not that it makes much difference now, but I feel like it's good to have closure and to air these things out, so we can both let go and move on."

"Yeah, Tess, that makes sense," Sterling agreed. "Let bygones be bygones."

"You got it, Sterling," Tess added with a sense of relief now that she had raised the question.

As Tess gathered her supply bag and packed her things to go, she turned her gaze back to Sterling, wanting to thank him for the brief talk. Funny thing though, she thought to herself, as she shifted her glance in order to do so, she saw him make exactly the same movement with his eyes toward hers. A stir of what she could only describe as affection rose up within her spontaneously, and she had to repress the urge that came over her suddenly to laugh and to smile.

"Bye, Sterling," she said as she walked toward the door.

"Bye, Tess," Sterling offered in return.

As both met each other's gazes again, they smiled, each happy to have finally broken the awkward silence about their past, and each pleased, perhaps even excited, about remaining on friendlier terms and seeing one another again soon.

Chapter 15

As the weeks passed and Sterling slowly started to heal, Tess's exercises for him grew progressively more rigorous. Knowing that Sterling's body needed both time to mend and challenges that would help him to regain his strength, Tess prescribed regimens of ever-increasing difficulty. At first they involved light repetitions of arm or leg movements or stretches. But with time, Tess initiated a new series of movements that took Sterling out of his room and even outside on the grounds of the vineyards. Using an electric wheelchair that could safely travel the paved areas, Tess soon had Sterling navigating outdoors, taking in the fresh air and the stunning views of the surrounding countryside.

On many of the trips with Tess and on other days as well, Mindy would walk alongside Sterling, trying to keep his spirits up with conversation and the presence of Biscuit, the ebullient new family pet. It had taken no time at all for the friendly mascot to work her way into everyone's hearts. Mindy, in particular, had embraced the new member of the family, taking charge of walking Biscuit daily and making sure that she was well-fed and cared for.

One morning, as Tess and Sterling were finishing the daily exercises, Mindy came by Sterling's room with Biscuit in tow.

"Sterling!" Mindy cried out. "Why don't we all go for a walk? You and me and Tess and Biscuit can all go outside and see how beautiful the spring is!"

"Hmm, well, I'm not sure," Sterling mumbled.

"Actually, that's a really good idea, Mindy," Tess added with a smile. "Sterling needs to continue to get fresh air, so that sounds perfect."

"All right!" Mindy exclaimed. "Let's go!"

Making their way outside with Tess watching Sterling's chair and Mindy leading the way, the group proceeded out the front door of the house and down the ramp Sterling's father had put in to allow him to get around more easily. With Biscuit enthusiastically setting the pace, Mindy, Sterling, and Tess moved down the driveway and out onto the narrow main road that wound gently through the sloping rows of vines as far as the eye could see. As they made their way further into the fields, Tess remembered that her next appointment was coming up soon, and so she excused herself and walked back toward the house.

As Sterling and Mindy continued their walk, with Mindy keeping watch over Sterling's chair and Biscuit ambling happily beside them, the siblings' conversation turned at various points to their respective plans for the future, the state of the year's grapes as they blossomed on the vine, and, eventually, to a topic Mindy had been wanting to bring up for awhile.

"Sterling," Mindy added with a smile, "I know I shouldn't be nosy, but what do you think about Tess?"

Feeling puzzled, Sterling turned toward his sister, not sure of what she meant. "Well, do you mean how she's doing as my therapist?" Sterling suggested.

"Well, yes, but I had something else in mind," Mindy giggled. "I mean, do you think you guys will get back together? You really are perfect for each other!"

"Oh, Mindy," Sterling exclaimed, "You really have a way of getting right to the heart of the matter. I mean, sure, the thought has crossed my mind. I'm not even really sure why we broke up in the first place."

"Well, there was the tiny matter of you kind of dumping her, right?" Mindy added with playful sarcasm."

"Actually, I didn't dump her," Sterling replied, "I guess we just kind of grew apart, and I'll admit that I probably didn't give her the kind of attention that she deserved."

"Um, yeah, Sterling," Mindy persisted, "and that's why you need to make it up to her. Here's your chance. Don't blow it!"

"I guess you're right, Mindy," Sterling sighed, "Sure, there's no guarantee that she would even take me back, but at least it's worth a try, right?"

"Exactly!" Mindy exclaimed. "Let's get to it, Sterling!"

Mindy and Sterling finished their walk as the sun started to make its way down over the hills in the distance, the rows of grapes bathed in the gleaming light. Sterling felt at once grateful for Mindy's uninhibited candor and nervous about what might await him with Tess. He knew there was no reason for her to take him back, and yet something told him that the hints of tenderness and affection he had sensed in their interactions over the previous weeks couldn't just be all in his mind. Still, there was no way to be sure. He would have to wait to see how things developed and when there might be an opportunity to ask Tess more directly about her feelings.

As it turned out, just such a moment presented itself a few days later during one of Sterling's physical therapy sessions. Tess had installed a railing along the wall in the exercise room, and Sterling's task was to use it to continue to rebuild muscle strength. Both his arms and his legs were now out of the casts, and his walk was improving daily, but his arms especially remained weak and in need of rejuvenating exercise. Tess had commenced a regimen to help, assisting him to hold on to the railing and then allowing him to use his grip to slowly make his way toward the far end of the room. This was a challenging exercise and Sterling dreaded it but knew it was what he needed in order to get better.

That day, about midway through the routine, Sterling could feel that both his legs and his arm were tiring out very quickly. He wasn't sure if he would be able to hold on much longer, and sure enough, before he could think about it any further, he felt his grasp on the railing slip away and his legs buckle beneath his weight. Sensing his body start to rotate, Sterling was sure he was going to hit the ground full throttle; but before he could react, suddenly he perceived Tess' grip around his waist, guiding him gently to the exercise mat and cushioning him from the fall. Safely seated once more on the ground with his legs and arms safely protected, Sterling could think of nothing else to say to Tess than a heartfelt thank you for saving him from what could well have been a major setback to his progress.

"Tess," he said as he looked over toward her, "I really don't know how I could ever begin to thank you for all you've done for me. You're really amazing at what you do."

"Thanks, Sterling," Tess interjected with gratitude and a hint of a smile as she stood up. "I appreciate that. It's my job, but it's also a pleasure to know that I'm able to help people. Now, if you'll give me your hand, I'll help you up and we can keep practicing your walking and arm movements."

Extending her hand, Tess noticed Sterling's hand rise to meet hers but then rather than getting up, Sterling remained on the floor, continuing to hold her hand.

"Sterling," Tess let out impatiently, "we don't have much more time in today's session. Let's get you up again so we can finish the exercises."

"Tess," Sterling interjected, still holding her hand and looking up toward her, "before you help me back up, I want to ask you if you would consider picking me back up in a different kind of a way."

"Um, do you mean you'd like me to go get the wheelchair, Sterling?" Tess added quizzically."

"No, Tess," Sterling said both solemnly and with tenderness, "what I'm talking about is whether you will consider picking me back up in a much more important sense—whether you'll come back, whether you'll give me a second chance, whether you'll forgive me for being such a fool for so long and for not seeing what a mistake it was to ever let you go. What I'm trying to say, Tess, is will you take me back? Even though I don't deserve it, will you give me another chance?

Stunned, Tess stood continuing to hold Sterling's hand, slowly processing what he had said. After what felt like hours to both of them, she finally spoke, surprising herself as the words "yes" and "I will" tumbled out. Though Tess too had been feeling something of a budding reconnection with Sterling in their weeks of therapy sessions, she had not had time to process her thoughts, much less decide to take him back. And yet, as if her heart and her mind both spoke in unison, she found herself assenting to the idea of entering back into a relationship with a person she had come to know in a different way in those weeks—someone who was still flawed, still human in the ways he had always been, and yet who had also been transformed in ways that intrigued and spoke to her deeply. Clearly, there were no guarantees of where this was all heading, but Tess knew that when her heart spoke it was best to listen, and so she did, helping Sterling back to his feet, steadying him with a smile and grasping his hand as the two walked slowly yet deliberately together toward the exercise room door and into whatever it was that the future might hold for them.

Chapter 16

THE FIRST FEW DAYS after Sterling and Tess's conversation passed with some awkwardness as the two reflected on their feelings and the words they had exchanged that day. Each felt some degree of reticence and uncertainty about how to proceed, but before long it was clear to both that something of the old spark between them had returned. For her part, Tess was realistic. She knew from experience that the real Sterling was far from the idealized version she had once imagined him to be. And yet the care she felt for him now was real, deeper perhaps than it had ever been before. She had seen Sterling go through the trial of his injury and recovery, and had witnessed firsthand the ways it had softened his character, eliciting an inner resilience not evident before.

To Sterling, the weeks he and Tess spent together in his physical therapy treatments had opened up for him a whole new appreciation of the woman he thought he had known. Though he had always felt attracted to Tess' sense of humor and independent spirit, he had not realized how genuinely kind she really was. Here was a person he knew he had hurt deeply, but who nonetheless showed up day after day to care for him. It was clearly not easy for her, and yet her humanity, her sense of dedication to her vocation of healing struck Sterling as nothing short of amazing as she literally walked by his side every step of the way toward his recovery.

By the end of the week after their conversation, Sterling and Tess had now reignited their affection, beginning to discuss where their relationship might be going and starting to think about what the future might hold. Sterling's time in physical therapy was quickly drawing to a close, and they would have to consider what to do. Would Sterling move back to L.A.? Would they have a long-distance relationship? Would Sterling go back to working at his company exclusively, or would he take his parents up on their recent offer that he take on the vineyard, but on the simpler, more modest terms they had always modeled? Neither Sterling nor Tess was sure where everything was leading, but during one of their conversations that week, Tess remembered that an event was coming up that might help to bring clarity to both of them.

"Sterling!" Tess exclaimed. "I just remembered that your parents told me on my way out last night that they want to hold a party in a few weeks!"

"Hmm, really?" Sterling averred. "That's pretty cool, but what's the occasion?"

"They actually want to throw a kind of celebration of your recovery—to recognize that you are back on your feet again, so to speak," Tess said with a smile.

"Wow, that sounds amazing," Sterling concurred.

"Yes," Tess agreed. "They're planning to invite lots of different folks, including from around here in the area, as well as some of the people who helped in your initial recovery down in L.A."

"Wow, I mean, they completely don't have to do that, but it will be great to see everyone and get to celebrate my return to civilized society."

They both laughed and nodded in agreement as they contemplated the gathering.

A few weeks later, the main house of the vineyard was festively decorated as friends and family gathered to celebrate Sterling's recovery and help send him off, likely back to his life in Southern California. Sterling was floored by the attention, and relished the chance to see so many family and friends gathered in one place. Making his way from one group to another, he was back in his element, the life of the party, the center of attention. In fact, as he made the rounds to the different tables set up outside in the warmth of the summer evening light, he seemed to grow less and less aware of his immediate surroundings. Immersed in the conversation and the attention, Sterling gradually lost track of where he was amidst the tables and guests. Not very concerned, he simply relished the attention as he moved from one place to the next.

However, what neither he nor any of the guests noticed as Sterling made the rounds was that he was drawing closer and closer to the edge of the deck overlooking the large pond that the tables had been set up around—the same pond, in fact, that Sterling had swum in often growing up, and from which, many years before, he had rescued his friend Ignacio, who also was present at the gathering with his sister Leti. Circling around to each guest and then continuing on to the next table, Sterling did not realize where exactly he was heading until suddenly, without the slightest realization, he rushed quickly from one table to what he assumed would be the next, only to find not another set of chairs with friends awaiting him, but instead the sun-soaked waters of the pond absorbing his body with a gigantic belly-flop splash.

Sterling instantly knew he had just made a gigantic fool of himself, but more than that, he sensed the beginnings of panic set in. Of course, he knew very well how to swim. And yet, would he be able to do so now? Could his still-weakened arms and legs move about under the weight of his clothing? Could he tread water long enough to make his way slowly back to the edge of the pond? All these worries and more came flooding into his mind as his limbs flailed around in the undulating waves his fall had set into motion.

Bobbing above and below the surface, Sterling felt himself slowly starting to lose consciousness. And yet at the same time he sensed his mind opening up and a vision starting to come together in front of him. At first, he could hardly make it out, but before long, Sterling could discern the outlines of a face. Indistinct at first, the face slowly started to come into focus, until Sterling at last let out a startled shout of recognition.

"Chris!" Sterling exclaimed. "Is that you?"

The face smiled back at him in affirmation, confirming that it was indeed the face of his friend that Sterling recognized. As if awakening from a dream, all of the scenes from his life and the lessons he had processed with Chris came rushing back to him. How could he have forgotten about such an intense series of experiences? How had he lost track of all the things they had talked about?

Sterling was anxious to start asking Chris questions and try to refresh his memory on all they had gone through together, but before he could get out his first word, the scene seemed to change again. Chris's face still remained, but now all around him things were starting to come back into focus. Slowly, Sterling realized that the face he recognized as Chris's belonged to someone who had waded into the pond and reached with a forceful grasp, pulling Sterling back toward the side. Gradually filling in the surrounding scene, Sterling could see that all the party guests had gathered around and were cheering as the man pulled him out, while several other guests joined in to help.

Now seated on a chair with a towel wrapped around his shoulders, Sterling still couldn't believe what he had witnessed. There was Chris, the same person who had helped him through what had seemed an eternity of reflections back on his life, now standing before him, and yet now Sterling knew where he had also seen him before. This was the same face he had awakened to in the car, and again as he revived from the coma, and who even been there all those years before when he had rescued Ignacio. In fact, he realized, it truly was one and the same person—someone his family realized had been instrumental in Sterling's rescue and so had invited to the celebration. And yet, in an important way, Sterling knew that this was his friend Chris, too. However you wanted to think about it, Sterling knew that his friend had somehow reached back to remind him of the lessons he had learned, hopefully now in a way that would last.

Sitting up with a bolt and then leaping to his feet, Sterling practically screamed out his recognition of what had just happened.

"I got it, Chris!! I know what to do now!!"

Startled, the party guests, including the surprised-but-bemused paramedic who had reached out to pull Sterling from the pond, stepped back as Sterling jumped up and down and began walking, then darting, then almost dancing around the pond as he took in deeply the consolation of recognizing what he was meant to do. Finally slowing down briefly where his parents, Mindy, and Tess were gathered staring in disbelief, Sterling took each of them in his arms and joyfully proclaimed what he now knew to be his life's calling.

"Mom, Dad, Tess, Mindy, and everybody," he exclaimed. "I don't have to wonder anymore. I know what I'm supposed to do! This is where I'm meant to be! I'm going to stay right here and run the business the way you always have. I know I'll never be able to fill your shoes, but I will give it my very best shot. I want to do what you have always done. I want to produce something of the highest quality in a place where I'm surrounded by family, friends, and a community that I care about and which cares for me. I remember why you named me, and I want to start trying to live up to that name. I want us, all of us together, to be the people I know we can be when we help each other out as all of you have done for me all these months of my recovery. I want to do my part to make our product and our lives what I know they can be—*sterling*!

With that, the crowd of partygoers let out a spontaneous cheer and burst into boisterous applause as everyone gathered around to embrace Sterling. As they embraced him, Sterling took in all of the love and let it flow back to each and every one of them. It had been a very long journey, and he knew that there would be many more challenges to come. And yet, as any winegrower knows in the fullness of time, Sterling intuited that, for that year, the vintage was complete. The grapes had blossomed on the vine, they had been harvested and processed, aged with the complexities of fermentation and patient waiting, and were now ready to bring savor and happiness to many lives. Sterling knew this year's vintage was indeed a distinctive one—one that stood out among all the others. It was one that he knew exactly what he would call—a name to mark the end of an old harvest and the beginning of something new; a name to call to mind who he had been and who he had discovered that he was becoming; a name to commemorate the unforgettable moments that had marked his journey of discovery. Sterling knew that this name would forever represent his transformation, that it would call to mind the extraordinary path of both shadow and light he had traversed; that it would ever remind him of the lessons that had graced his spirit in a permanent and indelible way—in short, that it would symbolize what in due season had finally come to pass, a rare and most precious gift: Vintage Sterling.